Praise for K. A. Mitchell's
No Souvenirs

"A perfect romance with stunningly vivid characters, a beautifully constructed plot, and a brilliant emotional arc. Everyone should go and get a copy. Right now!"

~ *Joan at Dear Author*

"KA Mitchell writes very compelling characters that have realistic baggage and issues that must be overcome."

~ *Rainbow Reviews*

GW00503697

Look for these titles by
K. A. Mitchell

Now Available:

Serving Love Series
Hot Ticket

Fragments Series
Life, Over Easy

Custom Ride
Diving in Deep
Regularly Scheduled Life
Collision Course
Chasing Smoke
An Improper Holiday
No Souvenirs
Not Knowing Jack

Print Anthology
Midsummer Night's Steam - Temperature's Rising
To All a (Very Sexy) Good Night

No Souvenirs

K. A. Mitchell

SAMHAIN
PUBLISHING

Samhain Publishing, Ltd.
577 Mulberry Street, Suite 1520
Macon, GA 31201
www.samhainpublishing.com

Editing by Sasha Knight
Cover by Mandy M. Roth

First Samhain Publishing, Ltd. electronic publication: March 2010
First Samhain Publishing, Ltd. print publication: January 2011

Dedication

For Sasha, an amazing editor who loved Scuba Cowboy from the minute he hit the page.

Thanks always to B.F.S. and Kathy. Yes, Bonnie, the Jetta is all about you. Thanks also to The Whistling Kettle for stocking the amazing Borengajuli Assam tea to keep me going all the way through.

Chapter One

The scuba instructor was destined for skin cancer by forty.

If Kim were a dermatologist instead of a trauma surgeon, he'd have dollar signs in his eyes at the sight of the freckled arms and back of the man assigned to give the scuba refresher course to the people going on the Sea Magic dive tour. Of course if Kim really were on his way to being a trauma surgeon, he'd be looking for a place to live in San Diego instead of getting ready for a live-aboard scuba dive vacation in Belize.

Kim must have lost his mind along with his chance at the fellowship at Sharp Memorial Hospital. It was the only explanation. He didn't make random vacation plans. Or any vacation plans. He hadn't let a vacation—hadn't let more than a few hours off—interrupt his careful plans to appease his parents' disappointment about the lack of grandchildren by becoming a surgeon. A surgeon who lived the width of a continent away so that they never found out he was gay.

Having a carefully structured life plan had been ideal—until Dr. Warren decided at the age of fifty-nine he preferred golf to heading up trauma surgery at Sharp. How was Kim supposed to have been prepared for that? His second-choice fellowship had to come through, even if it sent him to a less sunny part of the Pacific Coast. Dr. Emerson couldn't be retiring too, could he? Exactly how cold did it get in Oregon?

Calculating the eventual payment sun damage would exact from the freckled instructor did nothing to ease Kim's frustration at being forced to take this refresher course. The tour company made anyone who hadn't logged a dive in the past three years suffer through another round of instruction. Kim hadn't logged a dive since he'd gotten his certification in high school fourteen years ago, but he'd learned it the first time. Like differential calculus, molecular biology and organic chem.

After the scuba instructor finished helping a woman adjust the buoyancy compensation vest she was wearing, he turned around to look at Kim. "Thanks for joining us."

Even if Kim didn't really need to be here, it wasn't his fault he was late. They had sent his luggage to the wrong hotel and by the time he had that sorted out, there was the whole confusion over his name at the dive shop where he had picked up his rental. No, he was not a girl, and he was very secure in his masculinity, but that mask and vest wouldn't fit him even if he were inclined to wear neon pink.

"So can any of y'all tell me why it's important that y'all don't hold your breath when breathing compressed air?"

The guy might have been giving a lesson on a dude ranch. The lilt in his voice made cactuses and Stetson hats tumble out along with his words. Which in a less stressful situation might have been nice, because a tall guy in boots, a hat and dusty jeans, drawl pouring sweetly from a wide mouth, was the kind of thing Kim had been known to bookmark on his laptop. Especially when that cowboy parted with the dusty jeans and boots in the first thirty seconds. He could leave the hat on for the ride.

But finding a cowboy here, in a hotel pool surrounded by hibiscus-laden rain forest, was an incongruity Kim's brain was having trouble reconciling. That, the snide welcome, and the fact that as a rule people got on Kim's nerves had him answering the challenge in a tone that usually got people to back the hell off.

"Surfacing from even ten feet underwater while holding a breath of compressed air can induce barotrauma resulting in a pneumothorax. In other words, a burst lung. Messy, but not fatal."

"And painful."

The instructor was trying to scare his students into correct behavior, which might have been practical, but Kim couldn't ignore the medical error.

"The lungs don't sense pain. It's not until the damage is done that the pain results."

"But you're still talkin' 'bout pain." Scuba Cowboy wasn't going to let it go. "Thank you, Mister—"

"*Doctor* Kim."

He had the instructor's full attention now. Blue eyes— probably contacts—and sun-streaked red hair. Every genetic reason to minimize exposure to the sun. Whether it was in the cowboy's native Texas or here in the Yucatan. Lean face, but damn, cute nose, wide smiling mouth.

"Shane McCormack."

He couldn't be more Irish—except for the whole Texas drawl thing. But then Kim couldn't be more Korean.

"So *Doctor* Kim, you wanna remind these nice people what happens when you don't follow the dive tables and get all the nitrogen out of your bloodstream?"

Maybe it was the way the tropical sun was turning the surface of the pool into a thousand mirrored reflectors, because Kim thought that Shane McCormack had just winked one of his artificially blue eyes.

Kim got it. Scuba Cowboy wanted Kim to be his medical bogeyman. Which, given the audience of self-absorbed adventurers, would be fun.

"Severe pain is common in all stages of decompression sickness. In Type I, skin rashes and cyanosis may occur. Also pitting edema, where your skin is so saturated with fluid it loses elasticity and doesn't come back when you push on it. Like an impression on a wet sponge."

A woman wearing enough gold jewelry to equal the Gross National Product of El Salvador grabbed the arm of the man next to her. The pretty blonde who'd needed help with her vest wore an expression of horror. Shane looked amused. The crinkles around his eyes deepened.

The medical words were often scarier than the actual definitions. "In Type II, we see seizures, hemiplegia, dysarthria." He was getting to the scary stuff now. Scary enough that he'd paid for an extra night in the hotel to make sure he was able to fly without risking decompression sickness. "When you get the frothy blood coming out of your mouth, that's when it's really bad. Pulmonary, respiratory and neurological effects can be fatal without immediate treatment involving a hyperbaric chamber."

Kim hadn't had this much fun since the Halloween when he'd dressed up as Death and wandered through the hospital. Fortunately only three people had known it was him, and he had enough on them to blackmail them into silence.

"How much does that cost?" asked the man with the gold-encrusted woman on his arm.

"A lot," the instructor said. "Y'all have diver's insurance? Because most regular medical insurance won't cover it."

After terrifying them physically and financially, the

instructor put them all through drills, setting up equipment, retrieving a lost regulator and sharing a regulator. He made each of them swim down to the center of the deep end of the pool with him to demonstrate the skills, taking Kim last.

Finally Kim escaped the refresher class, only to have Scuba Cowboy track him down as he headed down the marina to the berth of the live-aboard scuba ship.

"That was fun," he drawled.

Freaking out the rest of the class had been fun, but Kim just wanted to be alone. "While it has been my life-long goal to offer you this brief moment of entertainment, I really just want to get my gear on board."

"Aren't you a prickly son of a bitch? Y'know, loading your gear is part of what you're paying the tour company to do."

"Am I also paying them to have you insult my mother?"

Shane chuckled and pulled the bag holding Kim's diving gear off his shoulder.

"Don't expect a tip." Kim took off down the floating boards, unsurprised that Scuba Cowboy's long legs could keep up even with Kim's fastest stride. Trotting down the dock would be undignified and probably pitch him into the water. He couldn't wait to get aboard. No matter how small the single stateroom was, he'd be alone.

When they reached the berth, Kim stopped abruptly. The trip might have been an impulse, but he had looked at the brochure, carefully calculated the square footage, and selected a cruise that promised a more stable structure of boat. But instead of boarding *The Sea Horse III*, the ship at the berth was *The Sea Glider II*.

Shane was already swinging on board, handing off Kim's bag to a steward. Turning back, Shane asked, "What?"

"That is not the right boat."

"Yeah, the usual ship is in dry dock after a run in with Hurricane Bradley. This is about the same, different layout, same number of berths."

The jump panic had induced in Kim's heart rate eased at Shane's words.

"Best part is, there's an extra bed with this layout so I don't have to sleep in the crew quarters. The chef's fucking one of the stewards and they're really noisy."

This was probably one of those male-bonding things Kim observed so frequently, the urge of all males, gay or straight, to talk about who was doing who as a lead-in to a discussion of their own sexual prowess. Shane might have been flirting with him or he might have just been making conversation. Kim had never had particularly accurate gaydar. His putting a mental tab on Shane as someone who'd look hot as hell on his knees with Kim's dick in his mouth didn't mean the opinion was reciprocated.

Shane jerked his thumb at the locker on the diving deck that bore Kim's name on a neon bright laminated card. Just like the first day of kindergarten. "I'll stow your gear for you."

"Thanks." Kim ground the word out from between clenched teeth and then headed for the guy with the clipboard to get directions to his stateroom.

Kim didn't believe in fate or luck. But as soon as he got to Stateroom B, stepped over the hatch and saw the bunk beds he knew. He wasn't prescient, just smart. Odd number, odd one out. He grabbed Scuba Cowboy's stuff off the top bunk and shoved it to the bottom. Kim was paying for the room; he got to pick the bunk.

Sliding the contract and confirmation from his bag, Kim reread what he already knew. "Sea Magic Diving reserves the right to substitute any part of the itinerary or accommodations due to weather or other circumstances beyond the company's control. There are no refunds."

Kim did have a clause that offered a "hurricane" check, entitling him to a tour on a different date if weather forced a complete cancellation. But that wouldn't apply.

"Well, hey again." Scuba Cowboy's red head poked through the hatch. That tall body took up far too much of the tiny space.

"You might have said something earlier."

"Didn't know."

Feeling trapped, Kim vaulted up onto the top bunk. The ceiling was so low, maybe he should switch again.

Shane suddenly seemed to get the idea that his presence was not only a surprise but completely unwelcome. The wide-mouthed grin turned to a thin line, shine in the eyes going out like someone had flicked a switch. "Well, then, guess I'll see ya at dinner." He ducked back through the hatch.

Kim stared at the entirely too-close ceiling. While they were still berthed, he should make the call he'd been putting off. Still stalling, he looked at his BlackBerry display. *Roaming.* No kidding.

Kim let out a quick breath of relief when Joey picked up. Kim wouldn't put it past Aaron to answer his boyfriend's phone—the controlling prick—and Kim wasn't in the mood for Aaron's sarcastic comments right now.

"Jae Sun? I'm so glad you called. We were worried." Joey's voice was earnest. But then he always sounded earnest. Like whatever you said was going to be so important he couldn't wait to hear it. The joys of a social worker's highly perfected bullshit.

Kim still didn't know why his hated given name didn't bother him when Joey used it. Maybe because the pronunciation was as dead-on as any of his relatives.

When he didn't show up for Joey's brunch, Kim figured someone might have noticed. "Yeah, well I'm sorry about this morning. I'm in Belize."

"Belize?"

"I just wanted to ask if you would bring in my mail and water my plants. That asshole you live with has a key to my place."

"Sure. I'd love to but...is everything okay? Why are you in Belize?"

That was the trade-off. No biting remarks from Aaron, but Joey wouldn't let him go without an explanation.

"I just wanted a vacation. Kind of a post-residency celebration," Kim lied.

"I heard about the fellowship. I'm so sorry."

Was there anyone who didn't know that Kim's entire future had just been fucked over? "Thanks for mentioning it. So you'll take care of the mail?"

"Sure. But what are you—?"

"I'm going scuba-diving."

"I didn't know you liked to dive. I've heard it's beautiful there. One of my exes said he'd never seen anything like the Blue Hole. We were planning to..."

While Joey went on about his ex-boyfriend's opinion of the diving in Belize, Kim amused himself by imagining what sort of remarks Aaron would have on the topic of a big blue hole.

And then he didn't have to imagine it because Aaron grabbed the phone. "The only hole I'm interested in at the moment better not be blue."

Joey's muffled laughter was still audible.

"Why the hell aren't you at work, Chase?" Kim should have called Elaine to pick up his mail. But Joey loved doing shit like this.

"I am at work."

"I wasn't aware that Shands Hospital was now providing fuck breaks for the paramedics."

"Maybe if you got laid more than once a decade you would."

"Please tell me you're not in an ambulance." Kim squeezed his eyes shut against the image.

"What I am in is a hurry."

Joey's voice came back on the phone. "I'll take care of everything for you. Mail, plants. Do you have a fish or a cat?"

Kim rarely had time to see the inside of his house. "No."

"How long is your trip? It sounds wonderful."

Aaron had the phone again. "Don't bring home any tacky souvenirs." Kim heard rustling, and he tried to imagine a struggle for the phone rather than what they were probably doing. Aaron maintained possession of the phone. "Talking on the phone is not at all what I had in mind for your mouth, Joey."

"Well, I'm not exactly getting what I had in mind for your dick either."

Or maybe they'd put Kim on speaker. He could just disconnect. He doubted they'd even notice he was gone. Pair of self-absorbed, love-sick idiots.

"Joey, could I just get five seconds?" Kim said as politely as he could.

He heard a brief struggle and then Joey's light tenor came back. "Okay."

"If anything comes from St. Vincent's in Portland—"

"Oregon?"

"Yes. Check my answering machine too. And then call me. If you can't get through on the cell, call Sea Magic Diving Tours out of Belize and get me the message."

"Sure."

The ship came alive with a low vibration that hit Kim first in the tiny bones of his ears. "Sorry, Joey, we're about to take off."

"Sounds great. Go yell *bon voyage* for me."

Even if this was the sort of thing where people tossed streamers off one of the three decks of the 120-foot yacht, Kim wouldn't be doing that. "I will. You'll call, right?"

"Absolutely."

The vibration grew until it was a bone-jarring rumble. "I've got to go, Joey."

"Have a great time."

"I'm sure I will." In a lifetime full of lies, little and big, Kim was sure he'd never told a bigger one.

The thrum of the engines increased, pressure building from the floor, through the walls and into his skeletal system until it buzzed along the sagittal suture in his skull. An inviting white pillow topped the iridescent blue-green bedspread on his bunk. It was only two thirty here, three thirty at home—twelve thirty in sunny San Diego—but Kim had been on a plane at five this morning. Not that the last decade of his life in med school and residency hadn't made him immune to sleep deprivation, but a nap would probably help his body adjust to the time shift and the motion of the ship. He took one of the prescription-strength antiemetics he'd brought and settled back against the pillow.

He had set himself to wake up in two hours, enough time to take a quick look around before dinner, but he woke up in less than half that, teeth and fists clenched against a wave of nausea. Seasickness wasn't something Kim had factored into his plans. He'd been on boats before and had never had his stomach so much as lurch. He'd even taken antihistamines to be sure his Eustachian tubes and sinuses would be clear on the dives.

He might as well have puked the four grand this week was costing directly into the tiny toilet in his cabin.

Chapter Two

Shane came up from the dive deck and caught a whiff of dinner. Familiar as hell, since it was the same menu every trip, but his mouth still watered at the spices, the sweet and smoke of the Caribbean-style food. First night out: chicken, beans and rice. Or for the adventurous, a bowl of sere and a grouper under mango salsa. Even if the chef was inconsiderately loud in close quarters, he sure as hell could cook. Shane could already taste the coconut milk fish soup.

If the cute but prickly bastard sharing his berth didn't haul his sweet ass up here soon, he'd miss the introductory slide show and piss off Alina, the tour's coordinator—otherwise known as the girl who was fucking the boss this month. Not that Shane cared, but then he'd have to listen to her bitch for the rest of the week.

As he headed back toward the companionway, the ship turned a little sharply and one of the stewards setting the tables looked up to the bridge. In addition to the different ship, they had a new captain. First run, Lord help 'em all. Popping 'round dive sites twenty miles off the coast wasn't exactly like tooling around Cape Horn with a raging storm shredding the rigging, but the captain had to watch it on the atolls. There wasn't much draft.

Shane tapped on the cabin door and didn't get an answer.

There wasn't anyplace else the guy could be. It wasn't that big of a boat. He opened the hatch and stepped through in time to hear the good doctor heave his guts into the head. Poor fucker.

He went down to the store—he couldn't get over having twelve tourists on a boat and the dive company wasting space on a store. But Sea Magic Dive Tours was completely committed to the magic of separating you from your cash so that you couldn't give the divemaster a decent tip. The expensive stuff was locked up, but not what Shane was after. He reached behind the counter and grabbed a box of acupressure wristbands and went back to the cabin.

There was a pause in the retching sounds.

"Hey," Shane called. "I've got something to help you with that."

Dr. Kim gripped the sides of the hatch as he stuck his head out. Shane had never seen that color on a guy before. He looked like dead coral, a nasty pale grey. Clipped words came out between clenched teeth. "While I'm sure you're willing to do anything in your power not to have to suffer the choice between the sound of me vomiting and the sound of the cook fucking, I've already taken something and I can't keep it down. Unless you have an ampule of Phenergan in your hands—"

"You don't take it, you wear it."

Whoa. Shane had never seen anyone arch their brows that high before. He held out the box.

Dr. Kim didn't lower his brows and he didn't take the box.

"They're acupressure bands. You put them on your wrists and this button thing pushes into your nerve."

"I can read the box, thank you." But the effort made Dr. Kim look like he was about to bolt for the head again.

"My sister wore 'em for the first six months of her

21

pregnancy. Only thing that kept her from living with her head in the toilet, she said."

"What a charming image."

Dr. Kim still hadn't taken the box, and Shane was starting to feel like an ass just holding it out.

He put his hand down. "Look, buddy, you want to spend a week upchucking, knock yourself out. I was just trying to help." To the tune of his pay being docked thirty bucks if they figured out he'd lifted the bands.

Dr. Kim stopped him at the door. "Wait. I'm sorry."

"No, you're desperate. Here." He tossed Dr. Kim the box, who fumbled before catching it. "Want me to show you or—?"

"I can find the median nerve in my wrist."

But with one hand on the box and the other gripping the doorframe so hard white knuckles showed under the grey skin, Shane wasn't too sure the guy would manage to get them on before he started tossing his cookies again.

"Give 'em here." Shane tore into the box and pulled out the elastic cloth bands. The doctor didn't resist as he grabbed the free wrist and slipped one on. Turning Dr. Kim's hand palm up, Shane looked for the pressure point on his wrist.

Shane's dick had been known to do the thinking for both of them more than once or twice. But it usually didn't express that kind of an opinion just from holding hands. The doctor was hot, yeah. Not particularly now when he was all grey-skinned but before, in the sun, when he was helping Shane terrorize the cattle, aka tourists. Dr. Kim's dark eyes held enough arrogance to tempt Shane into seeing what it would take to get him on his knees, and when they narrowed in focus, like the way he was looking down at Shane's hand right now, Shane wondered if a kiss would make them pop open wide.

So okay, the guy was hot, but not spring-a-woody-just-from-touching hot. Even if the hollows under the doctor's sharp cheekbones were giving Shane's brain a free-porn preview of how the doctor would look sucking cock.

Shane told his dick to calm down before they were out of a job. Again. He moved the band a bit and the white knob underneath sank in to press on the right nerve.

"I don't feel any different," Dr. Kim said.

Shane did, but he was trying hard not to. "Gotta have 'em both on for it to work."

Dr. Kim seemed reluctant to let go of the doorframe, but Shane just lifted his hand off and slipped the band on. This time when he turned the doctor's hand over it was Shane's upstairs brain that got the shock. A tattoo from some old metal band didn't seem to jibe with the pressed collared shirt and crisp khakis on the rest of the doctor.

Shane's memory finally produced a name to go with the ink. "Queensrÿche."

The doctor started to nod, then must have thought better of it and just said, "Yes."

"Big fan?"

"I was at the time."

It took more feeling around with Shane's thumb to find the right spot. Whoever had done the ink had laid it on so thick it was raised in the middle, but he found the spot just above the ridge. Damn. He'd kind of been hoping for an excuse to keep holding on, rubbing his thumb across the warm skin.

The solid muscle and bone in the strong but small wrist in his grip got his dick making suggestions again. Thinking back on the last time he'd heard a Queensrÿche song, Shane finally got it. Put longer hair on the doctor and get him to smile maybe

23

once or twice and he'd look like that yoga instructor Shane had been so inappropriately hot for. Damn. Every time Shane had tried to be in the present moment, the sound of that soft voice guiding him through the positions made his present moment all about imagining the graceful strength in that compact muscular body wrapped around him.

It was a relief to figure out what had him so ready to go. It beat the hell out of knowing his dick hadn't decided it preferred holding hands to fucking.

He settled the second band in place on the doctor's wrist and pressed on the button that pushed the disc down into his nerve. "Well?"

The doctor took a few deep breaths through his nose, and then unclenched his jaw. "Better." His tone rose in mild surprise.

"You didn't expect it to work."

"I didn't. But under the circumstances, I was even ready to consider voodoo."

"Well, the cook might have a chicken or two, I might be able to get a doll from Juan Carlos, but as for the fingernails, hair and priestess, you're going to have to make your own arrangements."

"But you'll be there for the ritual?"

"Unless I have other plans."

"Oh, of course. The demands of the high-impact career of divemaster must take precedence."

Shane should have been pissed. He did have something of a career as a marine archaeologist—when he could find an interesting project that was getting steady funding. But there was a glint in the dark eyes looking up at him above those sexy cheekbones. Dr. Kim had a dust-dry wit under that cactus-prickly exterior.

"Y'know, you're much less of a dick when you're grateful."

"Do you expect gratitude for that assessment?"

Shane laid his aw-shucks drawl on thick. "My mama taught me better'n t'expect the impossible."

The doctor stepped around him, tight body in tight quarters, and that got Shane's dick playing jack-in-the-box in his shorts again. He had to hook his thumbs into his belt loops to keep from reaching for his cranky bunkmate. After digging into his bag, the doctor came out with a bottle of water. Shane could've cleared the path back to the head, but he stayed right where he was and let the doctor work around him, the barest brush of the doctor's clothing spreading sensation like Shane would normally get from touching skin.

Last night's blowjob felt a lot longer than eighteen hours ago. And hell, it had been a lot longer since he'd had a decent lay. It was on the tip of his tongue to ask the doctor what his professional opinion on fucking guys was when he realized the doctor had stepped back out of the bathroom and was taking a good long look at the big-top tent in Shane's khakis.

"Should I be flattered?" Dr. Kim folded his arms across his chest, water bottle still in his left hand.

"Depends on if you care for the compliment."

"I do."

For a good long second, missing the soup and pissing off Alina for the next two rotations didn't seem to matter much, because he was getting his thumbs on those cheekbones, sharp as glass the way they could only be on another guy. The skin was smooth and warm, a sunny gold color chasing off the grey.

The doctor put a hand on Shane's chest. "But I'd be much more appreciative of the compliment if I was sure I could safely move more than a meter from an appropriate receptacle."

It wasn't an unequivocal "ain't ever gonna happen, son", and Shane couldn't stop his thumbs from tracing the bones beneath the skin, couldn't keep his fingers from sliding up from the base of the doctor's neck, into the spiky gelled tips of his hair. "Appreciative of the compliment? You talk like that when you're fucking, Dr. Kim?"

"It depends on the ride, Cowboy."

Shane's breath caught and he ran his tongue along the inside of his teeth to hide it, then let his tongue lick out at the corner of the smile the doctor kept pulling onto Shane's lips.

"Let me know when y'all are ready for a trip to the rodeo, Doc."

The doctor tried to give him a sneer, but he couldn't stop the smile that slipped onto his own lips.

"So, Doc, what's a guy call you in bed?"

"Definitely not *Doc*. Especially if he plans to get off." Dr. Kim's eyes were hard, but then he shrugged. "You can call me Kim."

Chapter Three

After half an hour with those bands on, Kim was forced to admit they worked. He'd managed to hold down a tablet of Compazine long enough to get it in his system and finally made it out of a cabin that was starting to smell like the ER on a good night. Of course, the improvement might owe more to the ship dropping anchor than to the voodoo of acupressure.

He made his way to the upper sun deck, the one farthest away from the bar, and found it blissfully unoccupied. The heat of the setting sun relaxed his muscles, soothing away the last waves of nausea, and he dragged in a few deep breaths of air untainted by air freshener, toilet cleanser and stale vomit. The breeze off the ocean smelled different than the one from the Jacksonville beaches. Smoother, but heavier. He lost himself in contemplation of whether the difference resulted from the salt concentration, the water depth or the proximity of the atolls and coral growth until his stomach sent up a distress call about its voided state. A calculation of the potential reasons for the different scent occupied his brain as he found his way to the dining area, only to be brought up short when he took in the seating arrangements.

The only empty seat was at a table for six that already held two young couples and Scuba Cowboy, planted right across the table from the vacant chair, his wide-mouthed smile putting fucking dimples in his freckled cheeks. When Kim realized he was staring at the other man's mouth, he looked away, but not before he caught the gleam in Shane's light eyes.

When the steward came over, Kim ordered plain rice, soup and a bottle of water. Everyone else at the table was drinking some local beer, no doubt because dehydration and hangovers were part of what made vacations fun to remember. The steward came by with another tray of bottles, and Kim hoped he wouldn't be paired with a still-drunk buddy on the dive tomorrow.

A glance around showed he was still the odd number which meant getting shoehorned as a couple's third buddy or having Scuba Cowboy all to himself. Kim wasn't sure his body was up for the suggestion in Shane's eyes, even if the way he put the beer bottle to his lips gave Kim all kinds of ideas. As had the flatteringly impressive erection. Kim had been certain that pasty and sweaty and reeking of bile, he'd have been the last person to inspire that reaction in anyone. But it had been a satisfying indication that he'd been right. Shane had been purposefully crowding in, finding reasons to touch and brush against him.

When the food arrived, Kim ate slowly and carefully. Vomiting in front of the divemaster was one thing, he certainly wasn't going to add the further humiliation of losing his dinner in front of all these vapid tourists.

The conversation—which consisted of Scuba Cowboy's polite where-y'all-from ice breakers and the couples' answers— was easy enough to tune out, even easier than the gossip at the hospital cafeteria. But that meant there was very little to distract him from an awareness of the man across from him and the easy smile on his lips. The more Kim watched that mouth, the more he thought of sliding first his thumb and then his cock over that soft pink curve. The relaxation induced by the sun and air vanished in a sudden rush of want.

Fuck if Aaron Chase wasn't right, the bastard. Kim did need to get laid more often. From the deliberate way Shane let his ankle rock against Kim's under the table, he was sure that barring further outbreaks of seasickness, he'd have the chance to spend a good chunk of time this week doing just that. It was almost enough to make him smile.

Excusing himself, Kim offered a polite if empty promise of a quick return to the blue-shirted female crewmember who reminded him of the orientation slide show scheduled after dinner, then made his way around the bridge and back to the empty deck.

The ship was close enough to Turneffe Reef to provide glimpses of circling and diving birds. With the engines off, the soft slap of waves against the hull and the gentle rocking induced the metronomic peace Kim had told himself he'd enjoy when he'd booked the trip. Or maybe the Compazine was just hard at work.

For a tall guy, Scuba Cowboy was light on his feet, but Kim knew it was Shane coming up behind him, even without turning. Anyone else would have been chattering away by now. The divemaster was a quick study. Among other more impressive physical traits.

Shane leaned against the rail and looked out at the reef for a few minutes before shifting around so that his back pressed the rail instead. "Can I ask you something?"

"I don't see how I could possibly stop you."

"If you hate being with people so much, why'd you come on a live-aboard? It ain't that big a boat."

"I did plan to be underwater or asleep most of the time. Neither requires conversation."

Shane snorted. "Guess not."

More silence, broken by the cry and splash of an osprey

29

making a surface catch and flying off to eat his dinner. Even with the sun so close to the horizon, the deck and rail held on to the day's warmth as a breeze from the cooler surface of the water chased away the humidity that made Kim long to trade Florida for California.

Shane spoke again. "So is it just people you don't like or the world in general?"

Kim didn't look away from the distant outline of the reef. "Since people appear to be a universal plague on the planet, I would answer both, but at this particular moment I'm inclined to cut the world some slack." He stared out at the spreading pink and purple from the setting sun.

He heard Shane shift to look in the same direction. Another cry came from the reef, a sound Kim could only describe as a seagull with a sense of humor.

When Shane broke the silence, there was no sign of a drawl, just a deep awed voice, vibrating against Kim's skin until he wanted to force the voice even deeper, hear a gravelly moan when he dragged Shane onto his cock.

"On the night dive, the colors are amazing. I never get tired of it. You lose so much of the reds and oranges from the diffusion on a daytime—"

"I am familiar with the principles of the visual spectrum, thank you."

Instead of doing what a sensible person would, take offense and leave or start an argument, Shane laughed, a far more pleasant sound than the gull's cackle. "Yeah, I guess ya are feelin' a mite better." His drawl thickened again. Obviously, he could turn it on or off at will.

"Why do you do that?" Kim finally turned to look at the man next to him.

The last of the sun's rays headed straight into Shane's face, and his lids lowered to shield the glare. The half-lidded look added to the air of lazy indifference more suited to a man leaning on a cattle fence than a ship's rail off the coast of Belize. Shane blinked, his lashes tipped with gold from the angle of the sun.

Lifting his hand from where it had been resting on the rail next to Kim's hip, Shane tucked his hair behind his ear before tugging on it. "What?" He dragged the vowel out until he sounded like a caricature.

Kim suspected Shane knew exactly what Kim had asked, but he said, "Put on that accent. Make yourself sound—"

"G'on and say it, Doc. Stupid? Like a tumbleweed rollin' hick who can't pronounce a word over two syllables?"

Kim didn't usually meet people who were as blunt as he was—unless he was meeting another surgeon over an anesthetized body. Shane's response almost made Kim drop his gaze, but he couldn't deny the accusation. "Yes."

"That's an easy one, Doc. I do it to piss off sons of bitches who think they're smarter'n everyone else. How'm I doin', hoss?"

"Rather well." A laugh slipped from Kim's throat, as unexpected as a hiccup. He gave into it.

Shane grinned, flashing deep dimples and bright teeth. "Damn, I wasn't sure you could do that. Thought maybe the muscles in your face got paralyzed some kind of way." His expression shifted, eyes widening. "And fuck. I know I shouldn't tell a bastard as arrogant as you are this, but smiling makes you the prettiest thing I've ever seen."

"I doubt that."

"Don't." Shane reached for him, lifting Kim's jaw with a big hand.

As Shane closed the distance between their mouths, Kim

thought of warding off the kiss. Thought about whether brushing his teeth had cleared away the bile, whether kissing a man in the open in Belize waters was what the guidebooks meant when they said that gay travelers should "exercise caution", whether he ought to make it clear that he was the one who made the first move, but it was too late.

Those wide lips were hot and firm and smooth as sun-dried silk. The tongue licking across Kim's lips, slipping inside his mouth, might as well have been leaving a warm wet trail down from his navel to his cock because heat flared along that line, pulsing right to the tip.

He didn't think anymore, just grabbed Shane's face and held him steady, deepening the kiss, stepping between Shane's bent knees to grind their hips together. Despite the way Kim's blood rushed under his skin and the sudden ache of need in his balls, the kiss stayed slow and measured. Shane didn't fight him for control, just met the rub and thrust of his tongue and the shift and glide of his lips.

The sun had slipped under the horizon when Kim stepped back, and they both drew in quick breaths.

"Damn," Shane said again, his grin coming easy, almost as lazy as his blink.

He stepped back, glancing at the sky, and Kim treated himself to another look at the solid length straining even the loose fit of Shane's khaki shorts.

"I hate to say it, but if you don't get your sweet self back to that slide show, Alina's going to have my ass. And believe me. That ain't at all what I had in mind."

Chapter Four

The slide show consisted of underwater photos interspersed with smiling people sporting Sea Magic gear—available for convenient purchase in the gift shop. As soon as it was over, Shane got roped into actually doing his job instead of the sexy doctor. Making nice with the tourists, checking gear and faking fascination with accounts of "really awesome" trips to Tahiti and Bora Bora took most of the evening and required more of the local beer than Shane usually drank. Maybe Dr. Kim was onto something with that leave-me-the-fuck-alone attitude. By the time Shane could escape to their cabin, Kim was out cold— or doing a damned good job of faking it. Neither activity was an I-can't-wait-to-get-your-dick-in-me invitation.

Shane kept a grumbled sigh to himself and stripped before sliding into the narrow bunk. Breakfast was at seven, the first dive at eight and he had to do another check of all the gear again at six.

Despite the beer, he woke a good bit before dawn with a dick that felt hard enough to club a shark. Given what he'd been dreaming about—Dr. Kim bent into positions that would have made Shane's old yoga instructor proud—the boner wasn't exactly a surprise.

He unkinked himself and rolled out of the bunk, stretching out the knots in his back. The guest beds weren't any bigger than the bunks in the crew quarters, but he already liked the quiet company better. When the doctor was there. Even in the dark Shane could see that the top berth was empty.

According to his dive watch, it was almost four in the morning and the moon was low in the sky, gleaming off the white hull as Shane came up out of the companionway on to the deck. He headed for the bow first to look on the sundeck, but there was nothing but silver light and grey shadows.

Moving aft, Shane found Kim stretched out in a deck chair facing the starboard rail, arms folded over his chest, dark eyes watching the sky.

"Something wrong with your bed?" Shane asked.

Kim glanced over and then back up at the sky.

"Or maybe you figured out you can't hardly turn over without hitting your head up there," Shane said.

Kim reached up to rub the back of his skull, lips twitching in a ghost of that smile he'd hit Shane with before. "Thanks for the warning."

"That's why I was going to take the top bed. Do I seem like the kind of guy who would put the paying guest in the bad bunk?"

Kim swung his legs over the side of the deck chair. "No. You seem like the kind of guy who would manipulate the paying guest into the uncomfortable berth with reverse psychology."

"Now that's giving me too much credit. But it sounds like you've come a ways from thinking I'm a dumb hick."

Kim stood, his body inches from Shane's, drowning the last bit of sleepiness in a rush of heat from that remembered dream. His dick started pumping like Kim's hand was already on him.

"That assumption was all you, Cowboy." Kim stepped around Shane to get on the rail. As Shane followed, their shadows leaned on each other and then slipped apart.

The moon hung somewhere between half and full, stretching a path of silver white from the boat out to the horizon, sharp enough on the still water to make you think you could walk on it. The itch started at the top of his spine, twitching all the way down to his feet, the familiar need to take off on that trail, find something new, something different. Like it always had, the need would keep rubbing on him until it felt like Shane would come out of his skin if he didn't go someplace else.

Fuck the money. Fuck guilt about having his parents bail him out again. He wasn't doing another week on this lousy dive tour.

Kim moved just enough that their bodies touched, a warmth of arms, hips and thighs pushing away the cool breath from the Gulf. The contact was enough to bury the itch under a fresh wave of arousal as Kim tipped his head up like he was looking for a kiss, but he only said, "It felt good sleeping out here. I think I've spent about twelve hours outside in the last eight years."

The guy had to be exaggerating, but Shane couldn't imagine spending even half his time indoors, locked up. "You must really have wanted it. The whole med-school/doctor thing."

"I do." There was something in Kim's eyes that said he'd give up a lot more than just fresh air and sunshine to get where he was going.

The look had Shane wanting that determination turned on him. Wanting to see what happened when Kim cut loose and started thinking with his dick instead of his head. Wanted it, yeah, but for the first time in his life, Shane had no idea how to get it. He'd never met anyone quite like Dr. Jae Sun Kim, never had a guy seem so completely indifferent to whether or not they hooked up. Shane might have thought the interest was all one-sided, except for the way Kim had been looking at him through dinner, like they were the only two people on the boat.

The hell if Shane was going to get all skittish now. If Kim didn't want this, he could open up that sweet mouth and say something. Shane reached for him, but Kim caught Shane at elbow and hip, yanking him around so fast he didn't have time to think before Kim dragged Shane's head down for a kiss.

Fuck yeah, it wasn't one-sided. Not with the hot hard thrust of Kim's tongue, the grip on the back of Shane's head that said he wasn't coming up for air until Kim was good and done with Shane's mouth. He bent his knees to press between Kim's legs, lining up their dicks for some good, slow friction.

But slow didn't appear to be on the menu. Kim's free hand worked between them. Damn, Shane expected a doctor to be good with his hands, but Kim had Shane unzipped and was teasing under Shane's balls with a feather-light touch before his oxygen-depleted brain caught up enough to think about reciprocating.

Kim never gave him a chance. He pulled Shane away from the kiss, hand stroking his jaw, thumb rubbing across his lip before Kim tugged Shane's head lower, a wordless demand Shane had given often enough himself.

Despite adhering to the dive tables, there must have been enough nitrogen left in Shane's bloodstream for a little narcosis because he had dropped to his knees, fingers already on the top rivet of Kim's khakis, before his brain hit on the thought that maybe this wasn't exactly the best place for a blowjob. And what the hell made Kim think he could put him on his knees like this anyway?

But there was a dark, shiny cock in front of his mouth, and

Shane wasn't going anywhere until he'd made Kim lose his fucking mind. Shane ran his tongue around the head, teasing a little more precome from the slit before rocking back on his heels and jacking the shaft slowly.

"So is this where you go all doctor on me? Tell me to lick your frenulum, wrap my lips around your glans, run my thumb down—"

Kim twisted a hand in Shane's hair. "No. This is where I say, 'Shut up and suck my dick.'"

Shane let the hand in his hair guide him forward, then rubbed his lips across the satiny head. Kim pressed his dick against Shane's smiling mouth. When Shane didn't open up, Kim pulled Shane's hair to tip his head back and asked, "What?"

"You didn't say please." Shane grinned and steadied himself with hands on Kim's hips.

"Shut up and suck my dick right the hell now."

Shane licked his lips.

"Please," Kim added finally, with a smile to answer Shane's.

Taking Kim deep right away, Shane let the thick head rub on the back of his throat, lips in a tight circle. Kim's grip relaxed, fingers petting and stroking through Shane's hair. When he pulled off with a noisy suck to trace the vein underneath with his tongue, Kim's hips bucked.

Beneath the deck under his knees, Shane felt the engines come to life. In about ten minutes the rest of the crew would be on deck. He and Kim were astern, so the captain probably hadn't seen them on his way to the bridge. Shane didn't give a shit anyway since he was kissing this job goodbye, but he kind of thought Kim's opinion on an audience would be a mite different. It was time to get serious.

Using a hand on the shaft, Shane sucked and flicked the head with his tongue. Kim's hand tightened in Shane's hair again, pulling hard enough to sting. Shane sucked harder, but Kim yanked his head away, triggering a perverse disappointment in Shane's gut. Yeah, they were in a hurry, and getting the reserved little doctor off so fast was candy-sweet to Shane's ego. But his body had just started flying on the taste and heat of Kim's dick sliding heavy on his tongue.

He tried to hang in for the finish, but before he could explain that he'd rather swallow than need a shower, Kim had flung Shane off and spun away to lean over the rail.

Shane climbed to his feet and stood behind Kim, listening to the breath whistle through his clenched teeth. Stupid fucker had taken off his wristbands. Shane put a hand on Kim's back and rubbed the tense muscles between the hunched shoulder blades.

"See now if you were sucking my dick, I could consider you choking to be some kind of compliment, but this might give a guy a complex. Something wrong with my style?"

Somehow Kim managed to keep from puking when he opened his mouth to spit out a "Fuck you."

"The bands don't work if they ain't on."

Kim gave a tight hiss of breath and then ground out, "Really?"

Shane remembered the other pressure point he'd learned and pinched Kim's earlobes, just under the cartilage.

The muscles in Kim's back softened as he leaned into Shane, and he tried to tell his dick that even if it had found a nice ass there to rub on, the guy was seconds away from tossing his guts over the side.

Breath a little steadier, Kim said, "My nausea turns you on?"

"Nope. Blowing you got me there, and your ass is keeping things warm."

Kim let out a shaky laugh. "So was this part of your divemaster training? Ten Methods to Conquer Seasickness?"

"Nah. I thought about being a massage therapist once. Took a course."

"Why didn't you stay with it?"

"Changed my mind. Switched majors three times."

Kim's body went hard and still against him. "You went to college?"

"I gotta tell you, the surprise in your voice ain't the kind of flattery that'll get you another blowjob. I did nine years of it."

"You make it sound like prison."

"Nope. Still be there if I could."

"And why aren't you?"

"They ran out of interesting courses, and I got tired of breaking in new advisors."

Shane swore he could feel the muscles shift as Kim arched those eyebrows all the way up to his hairline. Playing Q&A with the arrogant doctor was entertaining, and Shane might have kept it up, but the stewards would be on deck in a bit.

"The engines will stop when we get to the first dive site." Shane craned his neck and twisted his wrist to get a look at his watch while maintaining the pressure on Kim's earlobes. "I'd say about seven minutes. Where are your bands?"

"They're in the cabin."

"You might want to keep 'em on unless you're in the water."

"I think I'll be all right now."

"Don't watch the horizon. Or the water. Just keep lookin' at the deck."

"Got it, Scuba Cowboy."

"What?" But Shane's hearing was perfectly fine. Coming from the uptight doctor, that was pretty funny and damned fanciful.

Kim didn't answer, just turned back and gave him that smile, the one that could kick a guy in the guts, unexpected as it was on that sharp, serious face.

"Yeah. Thanks, Doc. I'm thinking you might want to make nice with your right hand since you obviously don't care if you ever get anything else."

"Oh, I think I will."

Kim made his way down the companionway before Shane could ask if Kim meant he'd be making friends with his hand or if he was sure he'd be getting something else.

The first dive made up for the rest of the trip, seasickness included. Unlike the spot near Tampa where Kim had been taken for his long-ago check-out dive for certification—a site visited by thousands of careless tourists a month—the reefs off Belize were as pristine as advertised, corals alive with color and life. Delicate purple fans, sharp thorny staghorn, intricate whorls of brain coral. A loggerhead turtle came by, showing as much fascination with the strange humans as they had in it before turning and paddling out of sight.

Since the buddy system was an inescapable safety ritual for diving, Kim found himself paired with Shane, though both of them spent the first fifteen minutes of the dive acting as photographers for the rest of the tourists. When the other divers became distracted by the sight of a small nurse shark, Shane jerked his head toward a large stand of staghorn coral. With one kick of his fins, Kim drifted over.

After beckoning Kim closer, Shane put a gloved finger on the sand near the base of the coral. Lips sealed around the regulator to keep in a gasp, Kim watched a fist-sized head poke out from the spines of coral. The spotted moray eel wound through the coral and emerged next to Shane's finger. If this was some bizarre game of chicken, Shane deserved to have the eel bite his finger off, but the eel just rubbed up against Shane's finger like an enthusiastic cat engaged in scent-marking. Shane made a bridge with his fingers and the eel rubbed all around, twining itself through with what looked like affection.

Shane waved and pointed down to the sand. Kim looked at his own fingers in deep consideration of the necessity for fine motor skills and intact digits for trauma surgery and then remembered how screwed to hell things were at the moment and why he'd come down to Belize in the first place.

What the fuck. Kim put his ring finger down next to Shane's.

The eel stopped rubbing on Shane's fingers and moved toward Kim's, stopping an inch away. The eel's pause gave Kim far too long to weigh how incredibly stupid this impulse was— as if the tattoo covering his wrist weren't reminder enough of how irrevocable some rash ideas could be. Then, soft and slick, the eel rubbed the side of its head over Kim's finger, moving as gingerly as if it were as uncertain about the whole thing as Kim was. It backed up and made another pass and then abandoned Kim for the evidently more pleasing rub of Shane's neoprene-covered skin, leaving Kim to wonder how many humans could say they had been snubbed by a moray eel.

The eel retreated under the coral, and Shane looked at Kim. Between the facemask and the regulator, it was hard to tell, but Kim was pretty sure the other man was grinning. They kicked their way back to the main reef for another session of photography.

Eventually even the other guests found something more interesting than themselves to photograph, and Shane led Kim away from the main reef again. This time he showed off a colony of anemones that fluttered like rapidly blooming flowers each time he waved a hand. Kim reached out to imitate his gesture, but Shane grabbed his wrist and pointed out a spiked branch of coral near Kim's arm. After a few brief signs, Kim nodded and carefully avoided contact with the fire coral as he made the brightly colored tubes open and close with a wave of his hand.

When they surfaced, Shane swam ahead to the deck and climbed out, turning to help the other divers adjust to the unpleasant return of gravity. Kim thought he remembered how heavy the tank and weight belt became after spending an hour weightless with buoyancy in the ocean, but when he tried his first step on the ladder, it felt like his tank would drag him back under. He took Shane's offered arm and got a wide grin in exchange.

The stewards helped strip his tank, ready with the promised amenities of a warm towel and the post-dive refreshments. The cold bottle of water was sweet after all that ultra-dry tank air and Kim had drunk half of it before he thought of the potential impact on his stomach.

As Kim retrieved the wristbands from his locker, he resisted the impulse to show them to Shane in the hope of getting that grin again, the one designed to make Kim think they shared some kind of secret. Keeping his back to the rest of the group, he slipped them on, pressing the knob of the button into his nerve with a thumb. Despite never having managed to acquire eyes in the back of his head, he felt the warmth of that grin on him. And then Shane was there, leaning on the locker next to Kim's.

"So what's wrong with Jason?"

Kim couldn't figure out who Jason was. Twelve years of reinventing himself as simply *Kim* kept him clueless until Shane nodded at the name above Kim's locker.

"Jae Sun," Kim corrected, adding the extra sound on the *e*.

"Still sounds a lot like Jason."

"But it isn't."

"You know what?"

"I know you're going to tell me."

Shane grinned. "I think you just like bein' cranky, Jay."

"Jae Sun."

"Okay. But Jay suits you. 'Sides, I feel kinda funny murmuring 'Yeah, Kim' in bed."

Kim considered making a distinctly Aaron Chase-style comment about Scuba Cowboy being all talk and no action until he remembered the blowjob fiasco this morning.

Shane reached down and took Kim's fins from his hand, and hung them in the locker, head bent close enough to drawl slow and sweet and sexy in Kim's ear.

"Yeah, Jay, just like that. Gonna make me come, Jay."

As Shane's warm breath teased Kim's wet ear, a flush ran from Kim's face on an express trip to his cock. Then the accompanying visual hit: Shane spread under him, that tight round ass cushioning the thrust of Kim's hips, Shane's face as red as his hair when he looked back over his shoulder to pant, "Harder. Gonna come, Jay."

Shane hung Kim's buoyancy compensation vest on the hook, his chin still hanging over Kim's shoulder like an overeager first-year resident on rounds. "Hmmm. Looks like those bands are really doing you some good. Lookin' pretty healthy to me, Jay."

From Shane's vantage point, it would be pretty obvious that

43

Kim's swollen cock would be wearing the imprint from the mesh of his swim trunks for the next hour.

It was definitely time to channel some Aaron Chase before Kim ended up getting rolled under a wave stronger than any he'd been upended by when Joey tried to teach him to surf. Kim stepped away from Shane and the locker, keeping his obvious arousal hidden under the suddenly too-warm towel. "Fuck. You."

One of Shane's blue eyes winked, and this time Kim couldn't blame it on a sunlit swimming pool. "We'll see about that, Jay."

Chapter Five

Shane was used to busting his ass on the dives, helping with the gear, pointing out where an octopus or a moray liked to hide out, taking pictures, all in the hope of getting better tips. Now he just took Kim to all the best spots, even if the only thing he wanted to get out of Kim was another chance to slide that surprisingly fat cock over his tongue and suck until Kim lost that better-than-you attitude right down Shane's throat.

Showing the good stuff to Kim wasn't about money, it was all about watching the tension around his eyes soften in wonder, like when Shane had coaxed out a diamond ray with the frozen shrimp Juan Carlos had smuggled from the kitchen. The ray huddled around for more of a free lunch, enjoying a rub across its pearly belly. Kim followed Shane's lead without hesitation this time, fingers gliding across the smooth, almost-velvety skin. Shane took off his glove and slipped another shrimp between the ray's hard gums. He joined Kim in rubbing his hand across the ray as it flapped around them. Their fingers touched, cool human skin rough after the slick hide of the ray. Shane locked his fingers around Kim's, pressing their palms together. The ray rubbed over their knuckles, but Shane was more interested in feeling the warmth grow between him and the doctor, the pulse of want beating under his skin as he thought about burying himself in the heat of Kim's body while surrounded by cool water.

He wasn't dumb enough to think it was possible under forty feet of water with full gear, but when they stopped at Lighthouse Cay on Wednesday, there was that nice little lagoon...

Fuck. They were going to see where this went if he had to lock Kim in their cabin.

Locking Kim in seemed like a pretty good idea as Shane considered his options after the midmorning dive. The tour had a picnic lunch scheduled on Half Moon Cay, where Alina would try to out-chirp the birds as she got all excited about Red-footed Boobies. The trip in the launch would make Kim sick, and even if it didn't there wasn't a spot on this cay Shane could think of that would be conducive to the kind of activity Shane had in mind.

Shane pushed open the door and every coherent thought in his head evaporated like water on summer-in-San Antonio pavement. Kim was stretched out on the bottom bunk in just a pair of boxers, gold skin everywhere. Shane would have drooled if he could work up enough spit to even swallow.

Kim's hand slid down his chest and rested over his crotch. "Going to shut the door there, Scuba Cowboy?"

Shane pulled it shut and locked it, resting his head against the panel for a second, wrangling up enough spit, if not sense, to get some words past his lips. "Don't you want to go to the cay? The Red-footed Booby is a very interesting bird."

When Shane turned back to face the bed, Kim rubbed his dick and hell yeah, Shane was going to start drooling now.

"You know, I've never really been into boobies." Kim kept stroking until a dark pink head peeked out of the top of those shorts.

"Uh. Me either."

So Kim wasn't indifferent. Shane was being seduced. His

confidence got off the bench, ready to get back into the game. He grinned at Kim. "But we'll miss lunch."

"Somehow I think we'll survive."

God, even that sarcasm of Kim's didn't do anything to slow down the rush of blood to Shane's dick.

"Yeah." But what was really running through Shane's head was *mouth skin fuck now.*

He took a step forward as Kim's fingers slipped inside of his shorts.

"I think you owe me a blowjob." Kim started to push down the boxers.

Actually, Shane thought it was the other way around, but he was kneeling next to the bunk and reaching for Kim's boxers before the next heartbeat.

"For Christsake, Cowboy, take off your clothes."

"Okay." Shane stood and yanked off his shirt, taking a little more care with the swim trunks he still had on. His dick was too swollen for yanking anything past it—except maybe Kim's smiling mouth.

"Damn." Kim reached up, smile growing broader. He ran a hand up Shane's arm, slid it across his pecs.

Shane had been tall for a good long time, but a skinny tall. It wasn't until the summer when he'd worked his first big archaeology dig that he'd packed on any size. He'd come home for Thanksgiving and his oldest brother, Mr. Perfect, the going-to-make-partner-next-year lawyer, had whistled and said, "Guess we can't call you little geek boy anymore."

He liked the widening of Kim's eyes even better than the hum of appreciation Shane was used to hearing from a guy when he took off his shirt.

Shane dropped down on his knees again, needing the taste

of Kim's skin in his mouth. He licked at one of the drops sliding down Kim's belly, found it not salty but sweet. Kim had showered off. For this. For Shane. Ignoring the roll of Kim's hips, Shane licked up Kim's chest instead of down, finding out just what Kim liked, whether he groaned more for teeth or tongue on his tits.

After winding up somewhere in the vicinity of Kim's pretty mouth, Shane lifted his head and looked down. Pretty wasn't going to cut it. Kim's cheeks flushed dark, teeth biting into that full lower lip, lashes lowered over his eyes. No. Not just pretty. Fucking gorgeous. Especially now when he was trying to pull Shane's mouth back to the warm skin that smelled like almonds and spice.

Now would be a good time for Kim to roll over. Shane could blow him later. Right now he wanted Kim going crazy with Shane's dick inside him. Shane gave a hard tug on one of those dark pink nipples then raised his head.

"Wanna fuck?" Shane's words put a stop to the eager motion of the body under his chest.

"I don't usually consider anal intercourse appropriate for a first date." With that dry tone in Kim's voice it was hard for Shane to figure if the doctor was fucking with him or not.

"Hate to break it to you, Jay, but we ain't exactly dating."

"Well, when you put it like that..." Kim twisted his way out from under Shane. The doctor's long fingers plucked a condom and a small bottle of lube from under the upper bunk. Someone had been pretty damned eager. "Roll over, Cowboy."

Shane ignored the way want clamped sharp as a barracuda's jaw in his belly. He didn't want Kim to fuck him. It was probably just shock. Shane's jaw had to be hanging open wide enough to catch flies, but he couldn't seem to do much about it. "Uh?"

Head tilted, lips curved in that way-too-sexy smile, Kim tapped his chin. "You've got a point." He glanced up at the overhanging bunk. "On your back would probably be better."

Kim had to notice Shane wasn't entirely on board with the plan. Shane had done his share of bottoming, back when he was skinny-tall and baby-faced. But since he'd grown into himself, guys had been sort of throwing themselves onto his dick. It was easy and fun and way less complicated. Besides, he'd be a lot dumber than he looked to turn down all the ass he'd been offered.

The doctor was just...hell, the guy would fit in his pocket. No way was he just going to spread 'em for—

Kim stood and peeled off his boxers.

Holy fuck. Shane had had Kim's cock in his mouth, but it had been dark and then there was the almost puking, so he hadn't exactly had time to form an opinion beyond *mmm, thick, hot*. Maybe it was a perspective thing, since Kim's hips were narrow and his pubes weren't bushy. Maybe. But Shane was thinking that for a little guy, Kim was seriously hung.

Kim stared dead into Shane's eyes and put a hand on that big cock, stroking it until it stood out straight, a little curve tipping the head toward his belly.

Shane's gut clenched with another shot of squirming need. That curve could definitely be a very good thing. He remembered how it felt, letting a guy take what he wanted, trusting him to get you there too. Of course there were the other times too, when the guy was just a total ass and didn't care if you got off. Somehow Shane didn't think Kim was that kind of guy.

Hand still working slow and steady on that dark pink dick, Kim waited. Clearly he wasn't going to try any convincing and just as clearly there wasn't going to be any discussion of switching things around.

Shane moved onto his back and let his legs drop open. If Kim said something obnoxious, this was all over, but those full lips didn't move. He just kept holding Shane's gaze, eyes heavy-lidded, teeth tearing into the condom.

Shane thought about how many years it had been and how thick Kim's cock was and prayed the doctor's foreplay went a bit farther than "On your back, Cowboy."

The deep rumble in Kim's chest as it came down against Shane's went a long way to quieting the anxious questions in his head. That groan said Kim appreciated what Shane was offering, the way he held Shane's head for a bittersweet kiss said Kim was going to make sure Shane appreciated everything he was going to get.

The tease and thrust of Kim's tongue and the heat of his breath kept Shane so distracted he didn't even hear the snap of the lube bottle before a slick finger was teasing around his hole. Suddenly he was no longer just going along with this, he was hungry for it.

The tip of that finger dipped, and his body pulsed with the memory of how good it was when someone did it right. He rubbed a leg along Kim's thigh.

Kim slowed the kiss, lifting his head, eyes fixed on Shane's face as he tapped and rubbed, until Shane wanted to grab Kim's hand and force him inside.

"We doin' this or what, Jay?"

Kim didn't smile, didn't make another comment, only raised his brows until they met the fall of his still-wet-slick hair, finger resting with just enough of a push to make Shane come out of his skin.

Shane bit his tongue against the urge to beg. "Need help? Should I draw you a diagram or something?"

Kim waited another second and then drove in, sizzling friction and perfect pressure. Shane's breath left him in a rush as Kim's fingers—please let it be fingers because if Shane felt this full on one, he'd never manage to take Kim's cock—set up a knowing stroke and rub until Shane's belly was full of warm honey, slick and sweet and smooth.

"My anatomy lessons were fairly comprehensive." Kim whispered the words into Shane's neck.

All that melting going on inside made Shane forget what the hell question Kim was answering.

Diagram. Anatomy. Oh. Shane took a deep breath, and it seemed to tighten his body around Kim's fingers. "My compliments to your instructors."

"Well, I did apply myself assiduously."

"I can tell." The fingers inside him did something that made Shane's dick feel like it had been swallowed by a hot, wet mouth. "Jesus. You must have—oh fuck—gotten straight—uh—A's."

No way. No fucking way was he coming already. Not with nothing but fingers in his ass and air on his dick. He could last longer than... But it was so hot, waves of it pumping from his ass to his cock, and Kim didn't waste a motion with that twist and rub and fuck inside.

"Jay. Stop. I'm gonna—"

"I know." An arrogant arch of brows and then Kim's mouth came down on Shane's, swallowing every moan as he bucked. He didn't shoot. God, how could he feel this good and not shoot, how could there be that much pleasure spilling over without it spilling out of his dick? And it went on and on, nothing but a few drops leaking like steam from the tip.

Shane had the feeling he'd have kept on with that coming-but-not-quite for as long as Kim wanted him to, and he couldn't help feeling a little pissed when Kim pulled his fingers back and rubbed lube on his sheathed dick.

Kim knelt between Shane's legs, and Shane tipped his hips up, half memory, half Kim's urging hand on Shane's ass. Kim shoved a pillow underneath. Shane thought about asking which bunk it was from, and then about which storage closet the spare pillows were in when the pressure hit, thick and hot. Trying to keep from either pushing Kim away or pulling him closer, Shane reached over his head and wrapped a hand around each bedpost.

"Fuck, Cowboy, that's hot."

He wanted his name on the doctor's lips, wanted Kim to acknowledge exactly whose ass he was forcing open around his cock. Since begging "Say my name" was too fucking pathetic, Shane only held on tighter.

"C'mon, Jay. Let's see what you've got."

But Kim had some damned good self-control, because even though Shane's body felt open and ready, Kim kept working the tip in and out until Shane was trying to swallow that cock with his ass.

The penetration never stung, never burned as Kim worked himself deeper. Just a good deep stretch, like hitting the perfect pose in yoga, muscles buzzing, tingling with awareness. And when he was in all the way, God, it felt so good to be full. Would be even better when Kim started the push and pull of fucking, when he worked the curve of his dick against Shane's gland.

"C'mon, move. Fuck me."

Kim shifted side to side, and Shane felt the strain in his neck as his head arched back.

"What's the matter?" Shane forced the words out with as much strength as he could manage with his legs in the air and a cock balls-deep in his ass. "Need me to beg? Is that what gets

52

you off, Doc?"

Kim's lips twisted and he looked up at the bed over his head. "I'm worried about hitting my head."

No. Not again. They weren't stopping now. "I'm starting to think..." Shane paused for breath, "...fate's got it in for us."

Kim bent down and pulled the pillow from under Shane's hips, palms cupping his ass. "I don't believe in fate. And if I did, I'd have to thank it for the interruptions."

Ouch.

Before Shane could gather up enough dignity to dish out an insult, or at the very least a demand for Kim to get the fuck out of him since it was such an imposition to have Shane's ass to fuck, Kim went on, "Because the longer you wait for it the better it is."

Shane shook his head. "I wouldn't know. I always eat the red jellybeans first."

Kim stared down, prompting Shane to explain, "My favorites. Delayed gratification ain't exactly my thing. So are you going to fuck my ass or not?"

"Oh yeah. And I'm going to change your mind too. Plant your feet on the bunk and hold on."

Shane braced himself on the bedframe, and Kim took a tight grip on Shane's hips and started to fuck with quick deep strokes that pushed the air out of Shane's lungs in groans. At the bottom of each stroke, Kim did this thing with his hips that sent shockwaves of almost-there, please-don't-stop shooting into Shane's balls and dick.

Shane had never had any complaints in bed, and Kim wasn't the only one who'd had an anatomy class, but this was fucking ridiculous. How the hell did anybody get that good? How did Kim know exactly what and where first time out of the gate?

Hitching himself up with his grip on the posts, Shane tried to fuck back onto Kim's cock while watching his face. Kim wasn't looking all cool and disinterested, but he wasn't exactly looking like he was about to lose his mind through his dick either. His face had a look of concentration though his eyes were almost completely closed, and a V-shaped flush spread from his neck down into his smooth, sculpted chest. When Shane tightened his muscles against the thick, pounding pressure inside, Kim's face softened, lips parting.

His eyes opened, and he almost smiled. "Ready for more?"

More? What more was there? Kim was all the way in, hips slamming against Shane's ass. And then Kim leaned forward, shoulders pushing on the back of Shane's knees, cock going so deep Shane would have sworn Kim was going to come out of his throat. Shorter strokes now, almost constant—Jesus, too constant—rub on Shane's gland. The hard muscles of Kim's belly brushed against Shane's dick, good friction but not enough. God, not enough.

Shane swallowed a sob. Kim leaned in farther, more skin on Shane's dick and yeah. So close. Things were tightening, his balls hiking up and the fucker stopped. Just stopped moving.

"Bastard."

"Let me."

Let him what? He'd let Kim top, let Kim toss his legs over his shoulders, let him in so deep he could taste him. What the hell wasn't he letting Kim do?

Of course the bastard had an answer. "Stop trying to anticipate everything and just let me fuck you."

"Will it get me off sometime in the next year?"

"Definitely."

The swivel in Kim's hips cut off muscle control to Shane's legs, but not to his mouth. His family always had said it had been a mistake to teach him to talk. The words came out as grunts, but they were perfectly clear to Shane's ears. "And when do you get off?"

"When you're a limp, sweaty, fucked-out mess."

Shane heard the challenge in Kim's voice and hell if he didn't want to meet it, but with that swivel, that liquid, unerring pump of hot cock on his prostate there was no way Shane could outlast the bastard. Wait till he had Kim in his mouth again. They'd see who was a whimpering mess.

Kim leaned down, forcing Shane's legs over his head, and kissed him in time with the thrusts into his body until Shane was a few seconds away from limp. Sweaty was already covered.

The rush up to orgasm was even sweeter, hotter, wetter this time, damn Kim for being right. With Shane's dick trapped between their bellies, there was just enough pressure on it to get him off, even if he ached for something more. He was so close it hurt, the worst hunger he could remember, a fucking canyon of want in his gut.

Nothing mattered but going over.

He angled his hips up to get more, more pressure, more cock, more Kim. With the hint of a smile that made Shane think he might have finally done something right, Kim slipped a hand between them and wrapped a tight fist around Shane's cock. So tight it stopped him mid-climb and Shane was going to cry. Cry during sex. Like a big fucking—

"C'mon, Cowboy. Gimme," Kim urged against Shane's mouth.

Kim's hand worked Shane's cock hard and fast, and it was a good thing Shane was quitting this dive tour because he knew he yelled loud enough to disturb every Red-footed Booby on Half

Moon Cay when that first jolt shot from his balls.

He couldn't have stopped yelling if his life depended on it. His hips snapped as each shot of heat from his dick sparked another, until it had to stop, had to, because oh fuck he was actually going to pass out from coming for the first time in his life.

Kim dragged it out, the hard jabs of his cock touching off more blasts of pleasure inside. Shane had been wrung dry but his dick kept right on jerking until it shifted into pain, and he shoved at Kim with what strength was left in shaking arms and legs.

Kim sat back on his heels. Shane should tell Kim he could finish fucking, come in his ass, but for once, Shane couldn't seem to find the words. All he wanted was to ride the aftershocks tingling his nerves into sated sleep.

The best he could manage was to let his legs drop open again and flash a wink. Kim shook his head and peeled off the condom. Smoothing his lips with his tongue, Shane watched Kim jack himself to orgasm, trying to see his cock and his face at the same time. Since Shane's coordination, even with something as small as his orbital muscles, was shot, he gave up and watched Kim's face. The look of intent concentration softened as his mouth opened and his eyes closed. He didn't make a sound, but watching Kim come was so hot Shane would have let him pound his ass for another hour if he could watch it again.

One harsh, barely audible breath and Kim shot a stream high up on Shane's chest. And again. Until between his and Kim's spunk, Shane's torso was covered with slick spots.

Kim rubbed his hand down Shane's belly, provoking a spasm from ticklish nerves. "You need a shower, Cowboy. You look rode hard and put up wet."

There wasn't time to nap, or even to lie there sticky and sweaty until they could do it again, and he certainly hadn't been expecting sugary pillow talk from Dr. Kim, but the accompanying slap on Shane's hip stung a lot more than it should have.

Kim swung off the bed and ducked into the bathroom.

Shane just lay there, ready with the excuse that the cubicle was way too small and he was just being hospitable in letting Kim have the shower first, since no way in hell was he admitting that he didn't dare get off the bed until he was sure his legs would hold him. As it was, he was thinking he might be as bow-legged as a ranch hand for the rest of his life.

Kim was out and drying off with a towel before Shane managed to remember how his leg muscles worked. "C'mon. I want you to ask that cute boy from the kitchen if he can smuggle us some kind of snack. We missed lunch and I'm hungry."

Kim waited to see if Shane would take the bait. He did— just not in the way Kim expected. No snap of temper, no angry answer that just because he'd let Kim fuck him it didn't make Shane his bitch.

Shane rolled off the bed and stood in front of Kim, snatching the wet towel and using it to scrub their mingled come off his chest. After leaning in for a slow, soft kiss, Shane traced Kim's lower lip with his tongue. The sudden sting of the towel snapping against his hip made Kim jump. The guy was lucky Kim didn't bite off his tongue.

"Guess you should have eaten my ass when you had the chance, Jay." Shane swaggered into the bathroom.

And Kim had been worried that Shane was too easy.

Kim loved a challenge.

Chapter Six

The cute steward came up to the bar with a couple of sandwiches. Kim accepted his with a "Thank you" and got an assessing all-over stare. He stared back, registering dark curly hair and what his romance-reading sister would describe as smoldering dark eyes and full pouting lips. The invitation in the steward's brown eyes was too obvious to ignore, even if Kim couldn't see anything smoldering, smoking or otherwise incendiary about the gaze. Juan Carlos was hot, clearly a bottom, and easy.

Easy was boring. Out of respect for the sandwiches—and any other favors he might need—Kim gave the guy a polite, maybe-another-time look in return. The lips pouted a little more, then Juan Carlos shrugged before walking away, a deliberate sway to his hips drawing attention to his perfectly round ass.

The sandwiches were filled with some kind of salad that reminded Kim of chutney. He took a bite and guessed that it was based on chicken, but with all that spice, it could have been almost anything.

Shane put his sandwich on the bar and stepped behind, coming up with two bottles that immediately began to sweat in the heat.

Kim read over the beer's label and then uncapped it.

"I get it," Shane said unexpectedly.

"Get what?"

"The way you inspected the sandwich, the beer, Juan Carlos. Fastidious, ain't ya? No wonder it took you so long to get in my ass. It had to pass inspection."

Kim hid a smile in another bite of chutney and thick wheat bread. "And I know you are profoundly grateful it did pass," he said around his mouthful.

"I can see you aren't suffering from low self-esteem."

"Or penis envy."

Shane gave a low deep chuckle, the sound traveling far inside Kim's ears, vibration tickling under his skin like a kiss on the back of his neck.

"You are quite a piece of work, Jay."

"Are you going to call me that out of bed now too?"

Shane leaned back against the bar. "It sounds to me like you think this is going to be an ongoing thing."

"I wonder what made me think that. Could it be the 'God, don't ever stop' or 'So fucking good'?"

"I never said that."

Kim arched his brows.

Shane took a long swallow of beer. "Actually, I think it was 'Oh Jesus, don't ever fucking stop.'"

"I stand corrected."

After a quick glance around, Shane bent forward and gave Kim a beery kiss. "You know I can't skip any of the dives."

Kim slid his hand around to cup and lift Shane's ass, provoking a groan from Shane's throat. "As sweet as it was, I really didn't pay four grand to fuck your ass, Cowboy. I'm not missing any dives either."

"Guess I'll have to make sure to get to bed early."

At dinner, Kim fended off another overture from Juan Carlos. The steward helped him with his napkin, placing it in his lap and offering a bonus grope. Kim would never blame a guy for trying, not one as cute as Juan Carlos, and Kim *had* held eye contact a little long when the guy picked up his napkin. Kim moved the inquisitive fingers off his dick.

Juan Carlos didn't appear insulted. He just winked and stepped away.

Jesus, the whole gay population of Jacksonville to choose from and Kim hadn't had a decent lay in months, so now willing men were crawling out of the woodwork on this tiny boat? Under other circumstances, Juan Carlos would be a pleasant diversion, but Kim was otherwise occupied with the entertaining process of teaching an alpha male he really wanted to roll over and beg for a dick in his ass.

Kim had been accused of mountain climbing by pissed-off sex partners and acquaintances. He took it as a compliment.

When the couple who'd been eating dinner with them excused themselves to change for the night dive, Shane leaned in, arms folded on the table. "You going to take him up on it?"

Kim had never been interested in wielding jealousy as a weapon. It felt like cheating. "Would he be worth it?"

"Wouldn't know." Shane shrugged, but Kim could see tension in those broad shoulders. Maybe Shane had seen the rejection side of Juan Carlos's sexy pout.

"I'm not compelled to find out."

"Why not?" Shane was almost across the table now, weight on his arms. The diffidence of that shrug had vanished.

"I've found something much more compelling."

That earned Kim a blowjob up against the door of their

cabin, Shane shoving him against the thin fiberglass panel as soon as the lock clicked. Kim's breathing was already tight and fast just from feeling the strength in Shane's body pinning his own. Shane could lift Kim with one arm, and having all that power kneeling in front of him pumped his blood hard and fast.

Kim bit his lip to bury a groan in his throat. Shane wasn't taking him very deep, but he made up for it with enthusiasm and energy. Hot, wet, tight, and moving was usually all Kim needed, but he closed his eyes and thought about putting Shane on his back, straddling his cowboy and filling his throat with cock as Shane gulped and fought for breath. Kim pushed forward, just enough to get that reflexive gasp and squeeze. Then Shane moaned and the hum of vibration was more than enough.

Whispering a warning, Kim tried to push Shane off, but his hands just cupped Kim's ass tighter, Shane's groans snapping the last of Kim's control. His fingers twisted in Shane's soft thick hair to hold him as volcanic spasms sent Kim pumping into Shane's throat. The pressure eased, but the light flick of Shane's tongue chased a few last sparks from Kim's balls until he was forced to sag against the door and pray the latch held.

"That pass inspection, Jay?" Shane's voice was hoarse and knowing it was from Kim's dick made the sucked-dry flesh twitch again.

Shane rubbed a drop of come off the corner of his mouth, and Kim sucked in a breath. He tried to be safe and polite when it came to body fluids, but nothing was sexier than that shine on another man's lips, knowing he'd put it there, that the guy had wanted it, asked for it. Jesus, Kim had to get his legs steady under him before they went on the dive.

"It'll do for now." Kim dragged his thumb across Shane's swollen lips.

Shane climbed to his feet and moved out of reach. "I suppose 'for now' is the reason you can't stand up straight and you're still hanging on to some of my hair." He rubbed at the sides of his head.

After an initial reluctance, Kim splayed his fingers wide, revealing the glint from a single red-gold strand. "How tragic. Did you need it back?"

"Un-fucking-believable." But Shane grinned as he said it.

They had about ten minutes before they were supposed to be on deck for the dive. Shane probably should be there in half that, but Kim doubted Shane would turn down an orgasm. With a push from the door for momentum, Kim used a hand on Shane's elbow to aim him at the bunk, reaching for his dick with the other hand. Kim's fingers had just brushed that tempting bulge when Shane knocked his hand away.

"Don't worry about me, Doc. 'Sides, thought you were all about delayed gratification." Shane pinned Kim against the post at the foot of the bunk, forcing a bitter salt kiss on his lips, tongue sweeping through his mouth until Kim's legs started to lose muscle function again. Being knocked off *his* feet wasn't the way things were supposed to go.

Shane stepped back and adjusted his jeans around the hard length that Kim had just imagined sliding between his own lips. "Don't be late for the dive. After all, you spent four grand on this trip."

Kim thought he knew what to expect on the night dive. But the sheer black walls that swallowed up their lights, the eerie sight of the other divers floating in empty space with glow sticks on their tanks, even the sudden appearance of a lobster scuttling on spidery spindled legs gave the whole experience a dreamlike quality.

His stomach lurched but not with the familiar tilt of motion sickness. The darkness was solid and impenetrable, the surreal sensory input disjointed, almost impossible to categorize. He didn't like it.

Light splashed across the coral next to him, sending more lobsters skittering for cover. And then Shane filled the black space next to Kim, solid and real, bright hair floating around his head.

Kim's jaw relaxed on the regulator in his mouth, and he followed the wave of Shane's arm toward a stand of sea grass.

Kim should have taken it easy on Shane that night. Should have done something nice and gentle to keep him off balance, like a long, slow grind. Kim didn't get off on dealing out pain, and fucking a guy who hadn't been done in awhile twice in twelve hours was pushing it.

He could rationalize it. If he was going to get to the top of this particular mountain, he had less than a week to get it done. And Shane had crawled into bed and shoved his ass right up against Kim's dick. But rationalizations were pathetic excuses wrapped up in nice psychoanalysis. The reason why Shane was muffling a groan in the pillow as Kim stretched his ass around a rough thumb was because that dive, that endless empty void, had left Kim wanting more than just Shane's grin and that fucking nonchalance to find his footing.

Shane groaned again and fucked back onto Kim's hand. He pulled it back to let just the tip of his thumb pop in and out of that tight muscle, leaning forward to trace his tongue along the length of Shane's spine, stretching to mouth a gentle wet kiss on the cool skin at the back of his neck.

Shane shuddered, hips grinding down into the mattress. "Come on. Do it, you fucking bastard."

Kim worked his other thumb in, rubbing and pulling and coaxing Shane's muscle to softness. The big body jerked, and Kim sucked hard on Shane's neck, tasting salt and the metallic edge of blood under the skin. Shane rolled like a wave under him, breath sliding out in whispered *yeah*s.

The bunk loomed too close to Kim's head, so he tipped them onto their sides. Hand on Shane's wrist, Kim squirted lube into Shane's palm and guided it between his legs onto Kim's sheathed dick.

"Put it in."

Even hidden behind Shane's plate-sized scapula, Kim could hear that grin.

"Hell, Jay, why do I have to do all the work?"

"Because I'm the guest, remember?"

Shane's hand moved in steady jerks on Kim's dick, spreading lube, dragging on the tight skin, thumb tickling the nerves under the head.

"Funny. I don't remember anything about this in the brochure."

"Then you need to get a new one." Kim lifted Shane's leg with a hand around his ankle.

Shane shifted, reaching behind until his fingers circled Kim's dick. The grip made Kim suck in his breath, but he didn't move. Didn't jerk his hips to get into that slick, tight warmth.

He felt Shane holding his breath too, until another wave undulated down from his shoulders and he worked himself onto Kim's dick.

"You goddamned sonofabitch."

"Uh-huh." Kim lifted Shane's leg a little higher and slid

home.

"Fuck." Shane's head dropped back, and Kim was glad they'd left the light on so he could see the sunset flush washing out the cinnamon freckles on Shane's cheeks.

The heat and the pressure sent a shockwave from Kim's dick to his spine. He shut his eyes to help hang on to the concentration that was swirling away with every clench of Shane's ass. Hips working quick and fast, Kim ran his thumb from Shane's knee, naming the muscles under the skin as he fought for control. He grazed the firm swell of the vastus medialis, increasing pressure along the long adductor.

Shane fucked back into him. "Harder. C'mon."

Kim moved his thumb in under Shane's balls, getting a sharper gasp. The drag of a nail on the thick ridge got a "God, yeah." But pressing that sensitive skin down until Kim could feel the rub on his own cock, yeah, that was the reaction he was looking for.

"Jesus Christ. That...fuck."

He pushed down just a little more, and Shane made a desperate whine.

"Like that, Cowboy?"

"Bastard." Shane reached for his dick and started jacking himself. "Stop and I'll fucking kill you."

Kim pushed up on his elbow and put his mouth on a sunburst of freckles on Shane's shoulder, watching his hand move in a blur as dark growls spilled from his throat.

When Shane came, he almost dragged Kim with him, muscles clamping around Kim's dick, pulsing with each spurt of white on Shane's flat belly. Kim lifted his head so his teeth sank into his own lip instead of the speckled shoulder, a cramp in his gut as he forced the hot flood back.

He managed to stay still as Shane panted through the aftershocks, locking their fingers together over Shane's dick as he came down, skin softening, slick as silk under their hands.

On a long exhalation, Shane's whole frame relaxed and sagged back into Kim.

"Y'can finish." Shane's vowels disappeared as the words ran together. "Owe ya one for that. Hell, owe ya ten."

Kim showed Scuba Cowboy a smirk as he reached over to grab whatever he could find to wipe off Shane's belly before urging him face down. Kim wouldn't be able to arch up as much as he'd like, but when he climbed on, Shane moved his legs together. God, that was tight, tugging and dragging on his skin even through the latex. He reached down and Shane grabbed his hands, holding them at his sides, fingers tangled together, tangled in the sheet. Kim wanted that moment where it all went blank, pleasure shutting down everything in his head, but he'd have given more than four grand to stay right here for as long as he could.

Because right here was almost that good.

Shane's hoarse gasps, the way he pushed back, even the painful squeeze of his fingers in time with Kim's thrusts had his balls filling too soon, and there was no pushing it back. He fought it so hard it almost hurt when he tipped over, when the heat was wrenched out, forcing his hips to snap against Shane's ass.

Kim's breath was still at hurricane strength when he eased back and flopped into the narrow space between Shane and the wall, abdominals aching, balls still tingling. God, they should do that again. Right now.

Shane rolled toward him. Their right hands were still locked together, and he pulled Kim's arm up until his knuckles brushed the bunk overhead, then settled his thumb over Kim's still-pounding pulse.

"I don't believe in love," Shane said suddenly, dropping Kim's hand.

Where the fuck did that come from? *Did anyone ask you?* But Kim's tongue was stuck to his palate while Shane explained.

"That song. I kept trying to remember that Queensrÿche song. Got played out on the radio that year." He tapped Kim's tattoo.

"Oh." And then he was up, glaring down at Shane's laughing face. "The single greatest sex of your life and you're trying to remember a fifteen-year-old song?"

Shane smirked. "I got kind of interested in what your hand was doing, and I kept looking at the ink."

"Kind of interested?" Kim arched his brows.

"Interested enough."

Kim dropped back down, not particular about where his elbows landed.

"Hey, Jay? If I admit I can't get my legs to work, will you get up and shut off the lights?"

Kim woke from a discomforting dream of floating in infinite black to the dark of their cabin. After a second his eyes picked out faint outlines, the only light a faint green glow coming through the porthole from the starboard light. The waves sent him rocking against Shane's heavy warmth, the same solid weight that had anchored Kim on the dive.

He rolled off the bunk. The deck tilted beneath his feet, but his stomach remained stable. He couldn't depend on a continuation of that happy state so he pulled on the wristbands again. He didn't like depending on anything, but at least the seasickness bands were something tangible.

The edge of the elasticized cotton landed just at the top point of his tattoo, a souvenir from his last vacation from common sense. Given that he was on a boat in the Gulf of Mexico instead of frantically tracing down another fellowship, he hadn't learned from that previous lapse in judgment, no matter how permanent the result. He ran his finger over the ridge in the center, worked into the design so it matched the Queensrÿche emblem on the *Empire* CD cover. At least this time Kim wouldn't be bringing any scars—decorative or otherwise—back home with him.

Maybe the vacation was what he needed. Getting laid regularly couldn't hurt, at least that's what he'd been told. In the meantime, he was going to take advantage of sleeping surrounded by nothing but sky and water.

He woke to a shadow looming over him and his lounge chair. Only Scuba Cowboy could cast a shadow big enough to have its own zip code, so it had to be him. Kim opened his eyes. Goofy grin, red hair and a big warm body. Right again. He shut his eyes.

"Whatcha doin'?"

Kim didn't open his eyes. "I *was* sleeping."

"Now why would you waste your four grand on that?"

"Perhaps I thought I needed the rest." He slitted his lids just enough to watch Shane's reaction.

The grin got broader, dimpling Shane's cheeks. "Wore out, huh? That's a damned shame."

"Fuck. You." Kim opened his eyes. "Oh wait." He smiled.

Shane looked up at the sky, where the nearly full moon was blurred by a ring of clouds. "Gonna rain tomorrow—today, I mean. Hard."

Kim glanced around the mostly open deck. "I imagine that won't be an inconvenience underwater, but what about the rest of the time?"

"Little claustrophobic in that cabin?"

Kim shrugged. He'd never particularly minded small spaces before, but so much of this one was occupied by tall, ginger and hot-assed, it was hard to think about anything else.

"There's a lounge," Shane said with a jerk of his chin toward the bow. "Under the bridge. It's small, but the furniture is comfortable."

And Kim was thinking about Shane over a black leather club chair, no more cramped bunk space, Shane's ass at the perfect height...

"Well fuck. Really?" Shane said, straddling the chair.

Between the lack of ambient light and the loose fit of the gym shorts Kim had pulled on, the twitch of his cock as it filled had to be invisible to Shane's eyes, but the man was staring down, running a tongue over his lips, an unmistakable shape pushing against his sweats.

"Really what?"

"You. All ready to go again."

"I'm ready to go back to sleep."

Shane shook his head. "You get this look, eyes, mouth. Jesus. Gets me hard. 'Cause I know damned well you are." He cupped Kim's balls, a thumb landing right over his thickening cock. "Yeah, you are."

Whatever Kim was about to say about involuntary stimulus response had to take a back seat in his brain as Shane moved his thumb up and down Kim's shaft.

Shane knelt on the chair on either side of Kim's thighs, and the lounge chair creaked. Kim was busy calculating their combined weight and estimating the chair's tolerance when Shane eased the waistband down over Kim's dick and stroked it fully hard.

Kim hung on to his concentration with what neurons were still under his control. The chair was probably rated for three hundred pounds, and they had to be close to three-fifty together. He could only hope the collapse wouldn't make too much noise because Shane had pulled his own cock free of his sweats and was rubbing it against Kim's, the thick ridges under their glans clicking against each other, bursts of pleasure firing along his nerves.

What the hell. He was on vacation.

The rub was good, blindingly, common-sense-numbingly good, but Kim figured it would take him almost an hour to get off with nothing but that electric pulse every time Shane moved. And then Shane lifted his cock, slapped it against Kim's, and he jerked his hips in response, back teeth clenched against a moan.

Wet friction now, both of them pumping drops of precome from their slits. It wasn't exactly playing safe, but Kim's forebrain was losing to his hindbrain in the Who Gets to Make Decisions race.

It shouldn't. This wasn't the kind of swept-away, up-against-a-convenient-flat-surface, fuck-or-die sex he could blame a lack of judgment on.

Nothing touched but their cocks. No kisses, no skin but that satiny slide and drag. But Shane might as well have been wrapped around him with his tongue on his tonsils with the way Shane's gaze licked at Kim's mouth and throat, the heat of Shane's body pressing against him from chest to feet.

This was payback, Shane needing to feel in control of

things. As far as Kim was concerned, it wasn't any different from getting a blowjob. He cupped his hand behind his head and rode the sensations with rolls of his hips.

Shane's mouth twisted into a grin, and he slicked his palm with spit before cupping their dicks in his big hand. One twist and Kim's body skipped over multiple steps in a male's arousal cycle to land squarely on oh-fuck-keep-doing-that-I'm-going-to-come.

Shane did, their hips picking up the rhythm. Kim could try naming every bone in the human hand as a distraction, but it wasn't going to do a thing to hold back the orgasm boiling in his balls. His body tightened and he opened his eyes to Shane's smile, a weird glow from the hazy moon spilling over his shoulders. Shane nodded, as if Kim needed his permission to come, as if Kim had a fucking choice about it when Shane's thumb rubbed under the head, hard and wet with that twisting tug on the shaft.

The orgasm punched through Kim's body, wringing tension from his spine, blotting everything out of his brain but the spasms of pleasure that drained his balls. Shane didn't stop, kept pushing Kim over that edge, finally easing him down with softer strokes. Kim's body still rippled with tiny shocks, but he caught his breath and managed to open his eyes again in time to see Shane's face tighten and relax as two quick tugs brought him spilling over his fingers. Shane rubbed their softened dicks together, slick and silky with come, a comfortable pressure, like the weight of summer warmth after all night in the frigid ER.

And no. This wasn't exactly on the safe-sex list, but it was a bit late to worry about that. Kim wasn't actually disappointed when Shane carefully tucked them both back under their clothes, but he wished Shane had just kept stroking them like that until Kim fell back asleep.

Shane shifted his weight off Kim's thighs. "So when do I get to tap this?" He cupped his non-sticky hand around Kim's hip, lifting him.

Kim pulled his legs free and sat on the edge so that he could lean against Shane, mouth against his ear. "I'm not wired that way."

With a flick of his tongue against Shane's neck, Kim lapped at the salt-spicy taste of his skin. As Shane arched his neck, Kim dragged the edge of his teeth against the skin, making Shane's body push closer.

"And you know what, Cowboy? Neither are you."

Shane made a snort that was more horse than cowboy and got to his feet, stretching against a sky that held a trace of light. "I'm going to do some yoga on the sundeck. You're welcome to join me, but I don't have an extra mat."

Irritation prickled under Kim's skin. Because he was Korean he automatically was an expert in anything Eastern? But he realized Shane was just being his usual friendly, boundary-overstepping, scowl-ignoring self.

Kim shook his head and climbed out of the chair. "I'm going to shower, maybe grab a nap."

"And no invitation to share?"

"I think you have a better chance of pulling an extra yoga mat out of your ass than squeezing the two of us in that shower."

"And yet we fit there." Shane jerked his chin at the lounge chair.

Kim glanced back. "We did."

"Kinda nicely too."

Kim's skin prickled again, not with annoyance, but with the tingle of pleasantly excessive sauna heat. Wanting to keep that shiver must have been his reason for prolonging the conversation. "How is it that a Scuba Cowboy finds himself doing Sun Salutations?"

"Damn, Doc, sounds like you've got me all stereotyped again."

Fuck Shane if he couldn't tell Kim had been teasing. He started for the stairs.

"Dontcha want an answer?"

Kim turned around.

"When I was a kid, I couldn't get out of my own way. After one too many trips to the emergency room, my mom decided I needed some kind of help before child welfare took me away. She was afraid I'd kill myself in karate, so she signed me up for yoga."

Four orgasms in less than eighteen hours must have torn through Kim's normally fine-meshed brain-mouth filter because "You ought to see my friend Joey," was out of his mouth before he could stop it.

"Yeah? He like yoga?"

"No, he's great at being a klutz. We're thinking of assigning him his own cubicle in the ER."

Shane nodded but his smile was gone. "See you at breakfast then."

Whatever had sent him off in a bad mood, Shane was back to big grins and teasing remarks as they suited up for the first dive. It didn't rain, and there was no picnic lunch, but Shane produced a key from somewhere and intercepted Kim after lunch, shoving him into the lounge, into what he was pleased to see was in fact a black leather club chair.

73

Before Kim could point out the advantages, Shane had Kim's shorts unbuttoned, smiling mouth sliding down Kim's dick. Kim sank back into the soft leather cushions. Shane probably wasn't going to lose the key anytime soon.

When the night dive rolled around, Kim debated staying on board. Three pairs of divers had decided to sit it out. Heavy cloud cover swallowed the ship's lights and the humidity was at a choking thickness.

It hadn't thundered yet, and there was Shane's wink and his promise of seahorses. The dive would only be thirty minutes because of the weather. Kim tugged on his rented wet suit and checked his safety gear again.

A single dive hadn't familiarized him to moving through the unnerving blackness and the flashes from the other divers' lights reminded him of the lightning they were all anticipating. But the sight of the seahorses, ignoring the spotlight as they danced out their courtship, was worth it.

Until Shane led them back to the spot where Kim thought the anchor line was supposed to be and it wasn't.

Kim started for the surface, and Shane yanked him back down, pointing at his regulator and the silver bright bubbles. Kim tried to free his arm, but Shane held on with bruising force, ensuring a slow ascent.

Embolisms, burst lungs, decompression sickness. Right.

Kim couldn't believe a moment of panic had driven the training from his mind.

When they got to the surface and the boat wasn't there, he realized that his previous sense of panic was entirely inadequate to the circumstance.

Chapter Seven

Shane scanned the horizon in all directions. He took out his regulator and pulled his mask off, letting it hang around his neck. He kicked himself higher on the surface and scanned again. There still wasn't any sign of the ship. He checked the reading on his compass, his dive computer, his watch. Right time, right location. He hadn't fucked up. They were where they were supposed to be.

The boat wasn't.

Shane's skin prickled even under the wet neoprene. A warning. A dread. Not his fault. Not this time.

Kim pulled his regulator out of his mouth. "Gee, something you said?"

"Can you put your sarcasm on hold for a second?" The weather hadn't changed, no thunder or lightning. "Inflate your vest, then the emergency sausage." The fluorescent float probably wouldn't be visible until someone got close to them. "You have that diver alert beacon, right?"

Kim switched it on. "Where is the boat?"

"It's not here. Could you put your regulator back in or something?"

In the on and off blink of the beacon, Shane saw Kim roll his eyes. The bastard was lucky that strangling him wouldn't help things. If it became even marginally useful, he would jump at the chance. Kim was acting like floating miles off shore with a storm coming was a minor inconvenience Shane had arranged just to piss him off.

The crew—the other divers—they had to notice that two people were missing. He might be Alina's least favorite divemaster, but he hadn't pissed anyone off so much that they'd try to kill him.

"I thought panicking was supposed to be a bad thing on a dive," Kim said.

"I'm not panicked. I'm pissed off." Shane was. This wasn't on him. Somebody else had fucked up.

Their buoyancy compensation vests would keep them afloat with minimal effort. They were less than half a mile from Turneffe Reef, where there was shore enough to sit on, if not civilization. They had to control their drift, maintain position and wait.

If the boat didn't come back for them—and if they hadn't been drowned, dragged south, electrocuted by lightning or eaten, they'd be able to swim to the reef as soon as it was light enough to see it.

"Can you swim?"

Kim had mirrored Shane in letting his mask hang around his neck. The flash of the beacon showed disbelief on his face. "Of course I can swim."

"You'd be surprised at how many certified divers can barely make it across a pool without the help of their gear."

"Shane." Not Cowboy. Kim's voice was calm, almost soothing, but still strong. The same voice he'd been using when he coaxed Shane's legs up around his ears. "Is there a chance we're in the wrong spot?"

"No." Shane's voice echoed back over the slap of waves. He had not fucked up this time. He wouldn't. Not with someone else's life on the line.

He pushed the anger deep into his belly and started planning. Drift was going to be the biggest problem. Especially if there was a storm. Being found in the open sea would be a lot harder.

Shane pointed behind them. "The reef is about half a mile that way."

Kim nodded, put his snorkel in his mouth and started to level off.

Shane grabbed him. "If we miss it, or if a current moves us south, there's nothing for miles. We'd be out in open water."

Treading water, Kim faced him. "I think I saw that movie."

Shane hadn't, but he knew the plot. Couple left behind on a dive. Lots of sharks. The end. "Well, we're lucky this isn't Australia. Not so many tiger sharks. Our problem is going to be staying in one place to be picked up." He thought of how long they could last if there was no sight of land when the sun rose. "God, and dehydration. I think I'd rather be eaten."

Kim grunted in disgust. "I think I'd rather not be picking options off that menu."

He seemed much calmer than he'd been under water. Shane wished they could have stayed under water. But the chances of drifting would be greater, and they'd run out of air in an hour or less. They were better off saving their tanks in case they had to use their regulators in heavy surf.

"I'll keep an eye on my compass. We can make a drag line with our weight belts." He looked at Kim's half wetsuit and ungloved hands. "I don't think hypothermia will be an issue."

"Speak for yourself," Kim said, but he helped Shane knot

their belts together and tie them to the small emergency buoy.

Of course this would be a great moment for Kim to say, "Oh by the way, I have a waterproof cell phone with GPS on it." But he didn't.

They floated.

Shane would have thought his first—and hopefully only— life or death moment would have been...interesting. At least not mind-numbingly boring. It would make a great story, whether over beers at a bar or over wine at the Thanksgiving dinner table, but the minutes—hell the fucking hours—were boring as shit.

Boring was one thing guaranteed to make Shane lose his mind.

Every so often he'd check his compass and they'd kick themselves north-north-west. As they settled back to float, he muttered, "'I am but mad north-north-west, when the wind is southerly I know a hawk from a handsaw.'"

Kim stared at him.

"Shakespeare," Shane explained. "*Hamlet.*"

"I'm aware of that. I did attend high school. But why are you reciting seventeenth-century drama?"

"Aren't you bored?"

Kim seemed to have to think about that for a long time. "I'm cold, hungry, thirsty and a bit concerned about the continuation of my lifespan, but bored, no."

Shane sighed and rolled his head around on his neck. The mask got in his way and he wanted to toss it away, but they might need it for something.

As they kicked their way back from another correction, Shane said, "You really don't mind floating out here with nothing to do?"

"There is nothing to do. That's what makes it peaceful."

"Except for the whole we-might-die thing."

"Except for that."

"And if it really is your last night on earth, you're all right with just floating in silence?"

"Truthfully, I'd rather have a mind-altering drug and an orgasm to see me out, but since neither is achievable, there's nothing to do but wait."

Shane considered how they could swing part two of Kim's request, but even if it would take his mind off things, it was better to stay focused on not drifting and not being eaten. They had to stay awake and alert.

"Tell me about your tattoo."

"Why?"

"Because I'm bored."

"Since when is that my problem? Amuse yourself."

"I'm trying." Normally, there would be books, or papers, or magazines, or people, or sex. Something else to do but stare at black water and try not to think of what would happen if morning came and they couldn't find the reef or the boat. What the hell was Kim doing that he couldn't make conversation? Planning surgeries in his head?

Kim looked his way as the beacon lit up again. "Fine. I got it when I was seventeen. It was a stupid idea. Permanent result."

"Why don't you get it lasered off? Get it turned into something different?"

"Aside from the pain and the expense, it serves as a reminder to never do something that stupid again. Apparently it failed." Kim fixed one of his arch-browed arrogant looks at Shane when he said it.

"What the fuck does that mean?"

"Hold your horses, Cowboy. I'm referring to the trip. I don't normally take vacations. I should have been smart enough to have learned what happens if you do something on impulse."

"So why did you?"

Trying to read Kim's expressions in the blink from the beacon was like trying to put together a puzzle with lots of the pieces missing. Like archaeology. Only harder. Right now, Kim's face was blank, almost bleak, none of the humor or superior know-it-all shit Shane was getting used to.

"I guess I forgot how much an impulse can cost."

Damned serious regret for a tattoo. But then Shane didn't have one. He couldn't imagine being stuck looking at the same thing forever.

"Then I guess it's good you took your sweet time checking out my ass. I'd hate to think fucking it was one of those things you regret later."

The bleak look was gone, replaced by that arched brow. "Fucking your ass was still a mistake. The Cheetos kind of mistake."

"Orange and crunchy?"

"A mistake to begin with, because then you want the whole bag."

"Well damn, Doc, you say the sweetest things to a guy. You must have a whole long string of 'em back home."

"I am string free."

Kim smiled when he said it, at least Shane thought it was a smile. He remembered the expression he'd seen on Kim's face when he'd mentioned his klutzy friend Joey. Kim's face had that soft happy smile, the one that hit in and around his eyes. Shane had only noticed it because it was so rare. He had no reason to be jealous, but he didn't like the idea of being fucked like that when he was just a substitute for someone else.

"So who's Joey? Boyfriend? Ex?"

There was that hint of something soft in Kim's eyes as he chuckled. Fucking chuckled. Who the hell was this guy?

"No, he's...he's just a friend." But the hesitation made it sound like Kim didn't know what to call him. "Joey is a force of nature."

"In a Cheeto way?"

"In the I-don't-have-the-energy way. And like most of nature's excesses, it's better to observe and keep your distance." Kim waved a hand out at the waves.

Shane hadn't noticed them getting bigger, but now he could feel them kick to stay on top of each swell as it passed. And he had no idea why he couldn't let the whole Joey thing go. "And Cheetos don't require a lot of energy."

"Seriously?" As he spoke, the wave lifted Kim first, taking him up a few inches so that he was looking down at Shane. "We're floating in the middle of the Gulf of Mexico on possibly our last night on earth and you're jealous of some guy on the basis of us having sex, what? Five times?"

Shane felt weird, ashamed and also stupidly pleased that Kim was keeping an accurate count. "Well, when you put it that way, I do sound like an asshole."

"And what other way would you put it?" Kim asked.

"I don't like being a substitute fuck."

"Cowboy, when I've got my dick in you, all I'm thinking about is...Cheetos."

"Well, okay then. But the big thick kind, right? Not the shriveled-up, small ones?"

"Right now, I'm thinking all the Cheetos are probably

shriveled up."

The waves were sharper now, drift spinning off to spray them in the face. It felt like a longer trip back to where his compass said they should be. As they started floating again, Shane rolled to look at the perfectly black sky. If there were stars, at least there'd be something to look at.

"So, if this is our last night on earth, tell me something you wouldn't tell anyone else."

Kim shook some water off his face. "I've never been to a slumber party, but I did listen in on some of my sister's. At the moment, you bear a striking resemblance to an eleven-year-old female."

"I'm bored."

"Again, I say why is that my problem?"

"Because you're the one who's stuck in the middle of the Gulf of Mexico with me on what is probably your last night on earth." Shane kicked up to match Kim's height on the wave.

"In that case, I think I'll just give in now."

Shane knew it was more of Kim's sarcasm, but raising the white flag didn't seem like Kim at all. "You would? Is that your thing? You just quit?"

Kim looked down like he was checking his watch, and his finger rubbed his tattoo. "Someone who quits doesn't make it through residency."

"And you did."

"I did."

There was a story somewhere, something interesting. All right. Shane had hours to pry it out of that pretty mouth. "And now what?"

"I need a fellowship in my specialty. I had one lined up in San Diego, but the head of the department retired."

"And you don't have a fall-back plan?"

"I didn't need one."

"Guess you did after all." It wasn't easy to score one like that off Kim, and Shane couldn't keep the grin to himself.

"I can stay at my current hospital. There's a position." Kim sounded kind of grim about it.

"What's wrong with that? I'm thinking if you picked it for your residency, it must be a good place."

"You don't always get to pick your residency."

"But you did." Shane didn't need to ask. Kim got what he wanted, Shane's ass knew all about that.

Kim nodded.

"So what's the problem with that position?"

"I don't want to live in Jacksonville."

"Who does?"

"It's too close to Orlando." Kim made the statement matter-of-factly, like anyone would understand the problem.

Shane thought it was a pretty weird reason. "What's wrong with Orlando—besides the tourists?"

"My parents."

"Don't get along?" Shane couldn't imagine not having his parents around, that safety net, a place to go to even when he didn't want to, people who knew him and mostly loved him anyway. That's what family was for.

The beacon picked out an amused expression on Kim's face. "We get along peacefully. From great distances."

"Should think they'd be proud, having a son who's a surgeon."

"That meets the bare minimum of expectation. I was going to be a doctor. There was never any choice there. My sister was supposed to be a wife and a mother."

"Oh." Shane got it.

"What?"

"They don't know you're gay."

"Considering the fact that they still acknowledge me, no, they don't." Kim's voice was deeper. Maybe because they were both having to kick harder through the waves.

"That sucks. How'd your sister turn out?"

"She married a dentist."

"Ouch." Kim didn't ask but Shane volunteered the information anyway. "My brothers and sister are all older. All fucking perfect. But at least no one cares what I do with my dick." No one except his sister that one time. When she set him up with her roommate's brother. *Shane fucked up. Are we surprised?*

After they corrected for their drift again, Shane said, "If you don't tell me something, I'm gonna just keep talking."

"Do I appear to have other plans?"

So Shane told him about the Taino site, how they were learning so much about the Pre-Columbian Gulf Coast tribes, but that since it didn't have anything to do with gold or mummies, but a lot to do with mud and fragments of cookware, there was never any funding. He left out the part where whenever Shane got on to something, it went pear-shaped. Funding, department closing, fucking the wrong guy...

Kim appeared interested, even asked a smart question or two. When Shane ran down, it was still a ways till dawn.

"C'mon. You've got to have something interesting to say."

"I see dead people."

Kim said it with so little affect in his voice, Shane could almost believe him.

"Really."

"Every day. There are a lot of them around the hospital. It's kind of nice because they don't bother me with stupid questions all the time."

"Dick. Of all the people in the world, I had to get stuck in the ocean with you. You are a major fucking pain in the ass."

"I'll remember to use more lube," Kim said gravely.

The predictable joke dragged out another question. One Shane hadn't been able to let go of with the way it dug in like a burr at the back of his mind. "Why'd you say that, about what did you call it, my wiring?"

"You know why."

Shane waited. Hell, there wasn't anyplace Kim could go to avoid the question. Shane might not know much about the arrogant bastard, but he already knew Kim couldn't resist a chance to hand out all the answers from his amazing brain.

"You like getting fucked," Kim said at last.

"Most people do. Feels good." He almost added *with the right partner*, but Kim didn't need the ego boost.

"I mean you like to get topped."

Shane opened his mouth to deny it, but even the ocean knew it was bullshit and slapped him with a mouthful of seawater.

The flash of light made the planes of Kim's face sharper, and Shane couldn't deny the sudden bolt of heat in his gut as he thought of Kim slamming into him, telling him to hold on.

"You like to get done. And you like to be told how," Kim said.

Jesus, now the asshole wouldn't shut up. Shane sputtered on an equal combination of ocean and disbelief. "I don't—" But Kim had already proven Shane wrong. More than twice. Fuck.

He'd have a better chance of redeeming himself if they weren't floating in the ocean. He'd get Kim ass up and tease until he begged.

"So what's your issue then, Doc?"

"I don't have one. I know what I like and I'm comfortable with it. Ergo, no issue."

"So you—"

"Really, there's nothing to it. There's no deep-seated psychological reason. I like to fuck guys. I don't enjoy being the receptive partner in anal sex, but I'm not opposed to giving blowjobs. Penises turn me on. Vaginas don't. Breasts can be pretty, but I don't particularly want to touch them. I don't like my feet touched. Is that enough or do you want the whole coming-out story?" Kim let go of the float to rub his right wrist over the tattoo. Maybe he was seasick and wished he had on the bands again.

"Hell, like you said, Doc, it's not like I've got other plans. Gimme the works."

Kim's head snapped around like he was looking at something. "What's that?"

Shane looked around. The waves were a bit calmer, the air thick. But he didn't see anything, no starlight, no moonlight, just the flash of their beacon trying to pierce that heavy darkness.

The sound built slowly over the slap of the waves, a throaty hiss, like a snake doing an impression of a lion. The sound vibrated into Shane's bones, a rush of too much water splashing down. He'd think they were on the edge of a waterfall but that wasn't possible in the middle of the sea. A splatter then, the sound of graveled hail on glass, and Shane's brain finally latched onto an explanation. For the sound. For the missing boat. He turned around, the next flash from their beacon blurring off a tower of shifting water moving toward them.

Waterspout. A fucking tornado made out of water heading right toward them.

"Dive, Jay. Get down as fast as you can without blowing your ears." He tugged up his mask.

Kim fitted his mask and slapped in his regulator. Thank God the arrogant fuck was as good at taking orders as giving them.

"Shit. Wait." The sound was something Shane never wanted to hear again, but they weren't going anywhere as long as they were still clipped to the emergency float. He dropped Kim's line and then his own.

Kim nodded as he let the air out of his buoyancy compensation vest, sliding under the surface.

Faster. Every pulse in Shane's throat screamed faster. He didn't bother with a look at the sky. He didn't know how much of the weird light was from the beacon or that crazy spin of water rolling down from the sky.

How far down? Could they get far enough down? The glow stick on Kim's tank was still emitting a faint green light as they dove fins up, Shane pushed his ears past pain, squeezing his nose when he had to clear them. Kim kept pace with him, steady kicks down. Any second a tornado made out of water was going to suck up this little spot of ocean. He checked his computer. Thirty feet, thirty-five, and then the bottom.

He turned to look up, but there was nothing to see. How far off had this taken them? Which way was the reef? Maybe they couldn't wait for morning. If they stayed down... He switched on his flashlight, checking for any familiar landmarks. There was the place where he'd shown Kim the seahorses. He thought. How many pieces of staghorn coral looked just like that in this part of the Gulf?

Provided the compass was still working—did a tornado fuck with magnetism?—the part of the reef with a shoreline was due west. Should they start out now? Five minutes ticked by. Shane checked his tank. Half. Holding his flashlight under his arm, he pointed at the tank and his gauge and aimed the flashlight at Kim. The beam reflected off his mask, a silver flash. Kim made a sign for half and then jerked his thumb up. Better than half. At thirty feet, that could last them the whole way to the reef, or not.

He looked off to the west, and then back up, as if he could get an answer from the darkness all around them. Another flash of silver, some fish swimming between them. Kim held out his hands in a questioning gesture. Shane held his hand out to say five more minutes. Kim pointed west. The guy had a pretty good sense of direction for being underwater in the dark.

An agony of indecision squeezed Shane's gut, his temples, his lungs in big lobster pinchers. Which stupid decision would kill them faster? Kim pointed his own light at him and then to the west and then at his compass. The giant claw still didn't let go. Kim nodded and started swimming. Shane let out a silver trail of bubbles and followed. At least if they died, he wouldn't have been the one to fuck up.

Chapter Eight

Air wasn't an issue. Light was. After fifteen minutes of swimming, Kim's flashlight weakened and died. He didn't know about Shane, but Kim wasn't about to try to keep his bearings underwater with no light. They could end up in Portugal.

Shane swam up, flashlight beam playing across Kim, just long enough for him to twist his wrist and check his watch. Four a.m. Eight hours in the water. His thighs ached from kicking against natural human buoyancy made even worse with the diving gear. Their weight belts—and the emergency float— were a casualty of the quick dive to escape the waterspout.

Shane pointed to his dive computer. They didn't need a decompression stop and they were only twenty-eight feet down. Still Shane's ascent was slow, and Kim matched him, ready to defer to someone who knew what the hell he was doing.

How the fuck did a simple vacation end up as a life-or-death endurance test? Because he'd fucking acted on impulse. On some insane assumption that any action was better than none and sheer forward progress would grant him an answer to his future. His future. That carefully arranged monotonous stretch of days toward the eventual horizon when the bio-chemical-electrical processes keeping his meat fresh would give out.

Maybe that horizon was a lot closer than it had looked this

morning. He was too fucking tired to care.

Dead meant not needing to figure out what to do when he got back to Jacksonville.

Shane and his light had moved five feet overhead, and almost without conscious thought, Kim's quads powered up a stronger kick, stiff tendons under the scar on his wrist tightening with the reminder. Dead wasn't the answer he was looking for.

Shane's light turned the surface to a silver mirror. As Kim followed the light to the surface, an irrational wish that somehow sunrise would arrive ahead of schedule stirred something as useless as hope in the back of his brain.

He broke the surface a few seconds later. It was brighter. The clouds had disappeared, leaving an almost full moon to spill light across the water and across the bright gleam of Shane's teeth as he grinned like he'd arranged the whole thing for Kim's entertainment.

"Look." Shane pointed west, or what Kim thought was west based on the last time he was sure where they were headed.

Kim pulled out his regulator and turned. First all he saw were whitecaps, then a patch of something different, lighter than the black water, rimmed with white and silver.

"The reef?"

Shane nodded. "Two hundred yards, maybe less."

Kim's legs felt a renewed burst of energy. He didn't care if it was a five foot square spit of sand. He couldn't wait to get out of the water.

Eight long minutes later, the reef beckoned like a mirage in a cartoon. Surf, sand, darker lines of sea grass and ragged moon shadows of palms. Kim kept staring at it, like it would vanish if he looked away. The burst of energy from seeing the finish line had given way to the burn of acid in his overused muscles. Maybe two more minutes and they'd be there. It couldn't be more than thirty yards away now.

Shane's breath burst from him in a grunt. As Kim spun to face him, Shane began a string of curses, breath tight and short. Kim was pretty familiar with all forms of pain exhibition in humans. He looked at the water. If there was blood, it was still too dark to see it. Kim's skin prickled, waiting for the teeth to sink into his own flesh.

"Move." Shane broke for shore.

Kim followed. "Shark?" Maybe they could still make it. Maybe the blood loss... Hell, they were fucked, but Kim had already decided he wasn't going down easy. He kept swimming.

Shane shuddered, breath coming in pants. He stopped, barely keeping his head up enough to gasp the words out. "No. Sting. Jelly or—siphono—fuck." He was lost again in a series of choked obscenities.

Kim shifted around to see behind him. He wasn't a marine biologist, but it wasn't hard to recognize the two oddly angular blobs on the surface. Even in the moonlight he could make out the bluish-violet tinge to the translucence. Portuguese man-of-war.

Shane had started mixing deities in. "Fucking Christ."

As long as he had breath to curse with, Kim was happy. It meant Shane wasn't in danger of any respiratory failure.

Kim could do this. Remove the envenoming object. Treat for shock. Man-of-war stings were very rarely fatal. Their venom was—what the fuck was it? This never happened. The information was always there. Kim never blanked. Damn it. Hemolytic or neurotoxic?

"Does it burn or throb?"

"F-f-fucking hurts. I—I—Jay—I don't know if I can make it."

In the last year, Kim had been mostly in the OR. He didn't have to put on a nice face for patients. He tried pulling out the firm voice he'd heard some ER doctors use. "It's a man-of-war. They aren't fatal. You'll be fine. Keep swimming."

Shane grunted, breath thick. "'Less there's ana—phylactic shock." His words were slurred like a victim of hypothermia.

"Do you have a history?"

Shane shook his head. "Shit. Hurts so bad I can't even...move."

"You have to." Kim doubted he could drag him far.

Shane kicked weakly, moving a body length or two forward. The jelly fish—*siphonophora*, the hyper-alert part of Kim's brain prompted—were left behind, but two blue tentacles trailed at the surface, wrapped around Shane's legs.

"We should get those off."

"Can't. Gotta swim before I can't anymore." Shane shivered, breath coming in thin gasps.

This wasn't like anything Kim had studied. He'd even done two cottonmouth snake bites in his first two years of residency. Antivenom? No. That was a box jellyfish. None for the man-of-war. The fuzz in his head was like static from radio stations competing for the same bandwidth. One stream had the clear, definite directions for patient care, but it kept breaking up under a panicked repetition of "Fix it, fix *him*."

"Anything numb?"

"I wish." There was enough of Scuba Cowboy in that wry assertion to take Kim's anxiety down a notch.

Kim fought the static, tried to tune in to the professional detachment that had always been there. Christ, he'd even diagnosed his father's heart attack four Thanksgivings ago,

92

forced an aspirin in him and driven him to the hospital while the rest of the family stood around having hysterics.

Just because he'd had his dick in Shane, thought he was funny and smart even out of bed didn't mean all his skills were for shit.

"We need to get those off you."

Shane shook his head. "Need out of water. Drag me."

Kim ignored that, digging through the files in his head for the one on siphonophora envenomation. It had to be there.

"Kim. Please."

Nematocysts. All still attached. And flooding Shane's bloodstream with venom.

He tried to get some force to his voice and found it in anger. "Shut up. I'm going to inflate your vest more." He reached for the valve and pressed it until Shane was floating high on the surface. After taking the flashlight from Shane's wrist, Kim peeled off one of his gloves.

Shielded by the neoprene, he yanked away the two trailing tentacles from around Shane's knee and calf. "Now. Slow your goddamned breathing before you fucking hyperventilate."

Shane's teeth clamped together and he nodded, but after a moment, he was shivering and panting.

His own teeth grinding together in frustration, Kim swam behind Shane, grabbed the back of his buoyancy compensation vest and started pulling. After a few kicks he felt the scrape of coral against his ankles and shins and shifted to his side, turning to aim for the nearest blob of land. As his efforts to get them to land destroyed several million tiny coral life forms, they exacted their revenge by cutting deep into his unprotected skin. He knew his shins were bleeding, but right then, exhaustion took more of a toll on his movement, dragging like lead weight on every muscle fiber as he hauled them closer to the small island. There was enough moonlight to see the edges now, and what faced them couldn't be more than several houses wide, but they wouldn't have to swim anymore.

When he could stand, he hooked his hands under Shane's arms and dragged him backward as fast as he could, hoping that none of the crunching underfoot was from fire coral.

Shane kicked again, getting his legs under him, and in an awkward lurching dance, they made it the last few yards to grassy, gravelly sand.

Warm. God, the sand was warm. Even in the chill of the predawn air. Despite the lumps of seashells and knots of grass, Kim found it as inviting as a pillow-top mattress with 1000-thread-count Egyptian cotton sheets.

But Shane still shivered and grunted, breath shallow and fast. The medical profession didn't make residents pull fifty-hour shifts for sadistic reasons, and despite the inviting bed of sand, Kim was up on his knees, checking Shane's vitals, stripping their heavy gear.

Shit. Respiration over thirty, a thin weak pulse over one fifty. He flashed the light over Shane's face. Lips grey, and when Shane blinked, his eyes were cloudy.

"Shane. C'mon now, Scuba Cowboy. Talk to me. Stay here."

Shane blinked again, and Kim shifted the light away. The blue eyes fixed on him and then Shane's gaze slid off. After a minute he focused again. "Got to get the rest off." He took a deeper breath. "No vinegar."

Right. Though whether Shane was warning him against the acid treatment or complaining about the lack was hard to say, but through the frustratingly opaque static a bit of memory filtered in. Vinegar, hot fresh water and urine are contraindicated in siphonophora envenomations. Rinse in saltwater and remove the still-active nematocysts by shaving or with sticky tape.

Saltwater he had. A razor was a little harder to come by.

He crawled over and found a large oyster shell for water. Next to it was a white fragment, shaped like an old-fashioned straight razor. Better than nothing.

He found a few other shells, filled them and crawled back. Shane's wet suit ended about four inches above his knee. The exposed skin was covered with thin whip marks, beaded and swollen, gelatinous pieces still clinging like clumps of cellophane.

Kim winced. That level of papular urticaria over such a large area of skin. He couldn't imagine the scope of pain.

Back at Shands Memorial's ER, Kim would have slapped a morphine drip on Shane the second he hit a gurney. He couldn't even let Shane lose the pain in a lack of consciousness because he had to keep his organs functioning. With cup after cup he washed the welted skin. The thick tangle of lesions might have been a nest of vipers writhing over Shane's leg. Dozens of lines, each of them full of hundreds of venom-pumping stings.

Shane wasn't even gasping anymore. Kim flashed the light on his too-pale face, called his name.

"Still. Here. Damn."

Kim looked at his makeshift razor. An abrasive paste would work best. He tried not to think about how much scraping that skin was going to hurt Shane. Causing people pain was an unfortunate side effect of a lot of medicine, but this was going to be like the fucking Dark Ages. Worse. Because he had to do it to a body he'd rather make cry out in pleasure, to a mind he'd rather match wits with, to someone who belonged on a very short list of people Kim called friends.

He filled the deepest shell again, mixing in sand to make a paste. He'd never been more reluctant to touch a patient. Shane shook silently as Kim patted it on, turning and lifting the injured leg gently to cover all of the damaged skin.

A choked gasp and then, "Gonna—"

Kim had become familiar with that warning early in his career. He shifted quickly, turning Shane onto his uninjured side while he choked out water and what was left of the long-ago dinner.

Shane sagged onto his back again, wiping his forearm across his lips.

"I have to scrape it off now."

"Don't want to know. Just do what you have to."

"I'm going to need you to hold the light for me." Kim put the flashlight in Shane's hand, wrapping the strap around his wrist and adjusting his angle. Shane permitted the manipulation with an alarming passivity.

Kim reached out and pushed the hair off Shane's forehead. "Hang in there, Scuba Cowboy."

"I'd fucking kill someone for some tequila."

"Yes, because dehydration and additional toxicity is exactly what you need."

Shane grunted.

Kim took a deep silent breath. One hand holding Shane's leg in place, Kim started with the largest area, scraping and rinsing his clamshell blade. Shane's breath whistled between his teeth and the muscles under Kim's hand vibrated, but Shane didn't vomit again, didn't even say a word.

Kim was doing the inside of Shane's knee when a hand shot down and locked around his wrist. "Wait."

Kim rubbed Shane's shoulder, realized he wouldn't feel it

through the neoprene and slipped his hand down under the thick hair to cup Shane's neck and rub the base of his skull. "Let me finish, baby."

Shane's eyes jerked open, the surprise in them clear despite bloodshot and filmy corneas.

Kim was just as surprised. He'd never called anyone *baby* in his entire life.

The corner of Shane's mouth quirked before settling back into a thin line. "Okay. Finish." A pause. A grunt. "Baby."

The pressure filling Kim's head eased. If Shane could joke, he was going to make it.

As long as he didn't go into respiratory distress. As long as he didn't go into deep enough shock that his organs shut down. As the litany of complications filled Kim's head, he almost wished the static back, as frightening as it had been.

He kept scraping carefully, removing every trace of his sandy paste before washing the injury in saltwater again.

"Any better?"

Shane shifted up on his elbows and looked down at his leg. "Fuck." He slumped back. "Not particularly, no. But it is better not to be swimming. So tell me, Doc, you call all your patients *baby?*"

Kim kept a constant eye on Shane's vitals as they waited for dawn. Human physiology was fascinating. Shane's body fought for survival, keeping his core temperature up, slowing his breathing, strengthening his pulse. Respiration stayed shallow and rapid, but his pulse had dropped gradually to one twenty.

He was still in severe pain, or as he put it when Kim asked him to rate it on the one-to-ten pain scale, "A fucking fourteen and a half." The skin continued to blister, welts thickening, darkening even as the sky got lighter, but he managed a few words of conversation now and then.

"I could scrape it again."

"Not until I'm begging you to kill me instead. Do you think you could swim for some tequila?"

Shane needed painkillers and an antihistamine. The problem with field treatment was knowing when you would better serve the patient by going for help. If Shane remained stable for another hour, Kim would swim to the larger island stretching to the west.

"They are going to look for us, right?"

"Hopefully they won't find the emergency float and give up, but yeah. They should. At least for a few days. Provided nothing happened to the boat."

"What do you mean?"

"If the boat ran into a waterspout and they find it wrecked with no survivors, they're going to think we were on it."

"Is there any habitation on that island?" Kim jerked his thumb behind them.

"Depends on which one it is. I don't exactly have a fucking GPS in my head, Jay. Can I sleep yet?"

"No."

After a minute Shane said, "All right. How big is this thing we're on?"

Kim stood and squinted again. "About half a city block."

Shane shut his eyes for a minute. "Sorry."

"Sorry you don't know where we are or sorry there's no habitation around?"

"Can you save the complicated shit for some time when I'm

not half out of it? Just sorry. Sorry you're stuck here."

"Why would you apologize for that?"

Shane's eyes took on the lazy half-lidded look Kim was learning meant there'd be nothing but a drawled joke in answer.

"Sorry for turnin' this into a workin' vacation for you." The accent almost masked the strain in Shane's voice. "Prolly think you're back in your hospital."

"I wish I were, because then I could drug you unconscious."

"Sounds good to me. Fuck. Hurts worse than when I caught a Duane Wojikowski fastball with my cheek."

"I begin to see why your mother signed you up for yoga." Kim stretched a hand out, fingers reaching for the hair plastered to Shane's forehead. It wasn't physically necessary and he wasn't sure if any touch would make the pain worse. Shifting his attention to the ground, he diverted his reach to picking up a broken conch shell and flinging it out into the reef. "So, are you still bored?"

"Fuck you, Jay."

At ten Shane was shivering again. His pulse got thinner, but stayed under a hundred. "Something ain't right."

Kim could see that. "Could you be a bit more specific?"

Shane let out a tight breath. "Could you be less of an asshole? I don't fucking know. Hurts all over now. Inside. Hurts to breathe."

Systemic allergic reaction? Shane's breathing was quick and shallow again, but didn't appear particularly labored. "Is your throat tight?"

"Not like that."

Kim pulled off Shane's other glove and checked the beds of his nails, the inside of his lip. Not exactly a healthy pink but not the bluish tinge of cyanosis either. He was getting oxygen. He prodded his liver, turned him to feel his back, his kidneys. Shane just grunted.

"Headache?"

"Yeah. Bad. And it's like a muscle cramp going on all in here." He waved at his torso.

He needed fluids. There was nothing he could do if the renal system was going to fail out here. Shane's eyes were tight slits.

It could just be a systemic reaction. It didn't have to get worse. Didn't have to be any of the horrifying possibilities Kim could call to mind now that the static had cleared. Shane's heart and lungs would keep functioning. There was no rhabdomyolysis in his bloodstream. No hemolysis.

But he was pale and sweating, and his breathing far too shallow.

"You have to take deeper breaths. C'mon."

He waited for another joke. Wanted to hear *Ain't you gonna call me baby no more?* To hear anything that would tell him this wasn't as bad as it looked. Shane tried, but the breath stuttered, ending in a gasp.

"You do yoga, for fuck's sake. Concentrate on your breath."

Shane reached out and squeezed Kim's hand, panting like a woman in transitional labor.

"Slower. Deeper. C'mon. Visualize or chant or whatever the fuck you need to do."

Shane squeezed harder, opened his eyes and managed one breath, but the next was tight. "Hey," he managed on the exhale. "Was fun, right?" Another breath. "We had fun."

"Christ, don't even go there with the farewell-speech shit. If you've got breath for that, you can keep right on breathing all the way to the hospital."

Shane closed his eyes, but his breath was a little steadier.

This wasn't from Shane panicking. Not anaphylactic shock either, though if it came to that, Kim would do a tracheotomy with a fucking shard of shell. Kim was angry. Not everyone lived, even with every advantage of the ER. But Shane wasn't everyone, and there had to be something Kim could do besides watch him breathe.

He was so intent on the motion of Shane's diaphragm, the whisper of breath across his larynx, that Kim only became aware of the mechanical drone when it filled the air with the sound of cutting blades.

"Helicopter." Kim yelled it in Shane's ear. There'd better be a goddamned medic on it with a basic IV kit. And then the thought came that they were two tiny dots on a bunch of other dots, and he jumped to his feet, waving.

"Signal," Shane grunted.

With what? Too late to start a fire. He held up an air tank, hoping the brushed metal would flash in the sun or at least make them bigger. He waved it, reached down and stuffed Shane's mask in his hands, angling it to get a reflection of light from the lens. When the helicopter turned toward them, Kim looked back down in time to see the mask fall from Shane's lax hand.

Chapter Nine

Shane remembered the sound of the helicopter, but that was the last of it. The next time he opened his eyes, he was in a hospital ward, gagging on the tubing in his throat. He turned to look for Kim and found a beeping monitor. A pink-clad nurse came over and smiled down at him, dark eyes looking genuinely happy. "*Bienvenido, Señor McCormack.*"

All he could do was gag on the tube until she held his jaw with one dry gentle hand and removed it.

He coughed out the taste of plastic. She dropped it in a nearby tray, and he glanced at it. Hell on a guy's pride. It wasn't that big and he'd always thought he had better control of his gag reflex than that, which had him looking for Kim again.

He thought about asking, but he couldn't seem to get his throat, lips and tongue to cooperate. He tried to raise an arm to mime drinking but that hurt too. "*Agua.*" It didn't sound like much, but she brought a spoon to his mouth and let him wet his lips.

"*Gracias.*" That sounded a little better.

She smiled again. He blinked and she was gone.

He might have been out for a second or for hours, but the next time he opened his eyes, his dad was standing next to him.

Shit. It must be really bad. He'd tried so hard to keep them from having to bail him out again, and now he'd dragged Dad to Belize.

"How are you doing, son?"

Shane licked his lips and eyed the cup of water next to his father. "Thirsty."

His dad held it for him. And maybe it was the way everything seemed to keep jumping around, but his father's hand was shaking.

"Thanks."

"I'm going to get your mother. There isn't a lot of room in here."

Shane's gaze followed his father past the end of his bed. There were a couple of other beds in his range of vision, each one holding an unconscious patient.

He knew what had happened to him up until the beach. He knew they'd been left behind. There'd been a waterspout and then a man-o'-war, Kim scraping the nematocysts off with sand, face sharp, lips grim and tight, but beautiful when the sun came up behind him.

Shane's mom told him they were trying to finalize a transfer to a hospital in the States. Even with the fog in his head he could hear her unspoken "real" in front of hospital.

After Mom, it was his brothers Josh and Braden. Only his due-next-month sister Megan hadn't made the trip. Apparently, he really had almost died.

Josh talked for about five minutes straight about Shane's excellent position vis-à-vis a lawsuit, and about contacting a colleague in international law since the dive tour company was based in the Caymans. The real moneymaker, Josh pointed out, was that after the captain fled the waterspouts, he didn't call them in as missing for five hours.

Josh was animated, the way he usually was around lawsuits, but Shane had to fight to stay awake.

Finally Braden shuffled in. Josh and his dad were big. Shane was tall. But Braden was huge, all-state nose-guard huge, a wall of solid muscle. A kick-ass Texas Ranger. And an absolute pushover.

"How long?" Shane demanded once he'd gotten Braden to let him drink.

"You were out until yesterday."

When Shane narrowed his eyes, Braden added, "Four days."

Wow. "What's wrong with me?"

"Nothing now, they hope. You had a reaction to the sting. They had to defib you on the way to the hospital."

"What could be wrong still?"

Braden looked over his shoulder.

"Tell me."

"They've been flinging some scary words around, dude." Braden glanced over his shoulder again before pulling his BlackBerry off his belt. "I checked some of 'em out."

Shane tried to get his hands on the phone and realized his arm was strapped down, fingers taped together. After a minute or two, he figured out he could raise the arm with the IV in it, but those fingers were taped too. He didn't remember anything happening to his hands.

"After you came out of the coma yesterday, you tried digging at your leg and the IV."

Shane tried to concentrate on his leg, to figure out when and if it was going to start hurting again, but all he could think about right then was *coma*. Jesus. That was a serious fucking word.

Braden held the BlackBerry for him to look at some tiny text talking about systemic reactions and then something about muscle toxins. It was all scary. But the fact that his head felt all disconnected from his body was even scarier right now. He wanted some answers that he knew wouldn't be bullshit.

"Where's the guy I was with? Kim?"

"The doctor?"

"Yeah."

"Don't know." Braden shrugged one of his boulder-sized shoulders. "He's the one who defibbed you in the ambulance. Stayed with you till they got you in ICU, even though he was cut up from something."

"Where is he now?"

"He checked on you a couple of times, read your chart, pissed off the nurses. But I haven't seen him since you woke up yesterday."

Shane's hand was reaching to pluck out the IV before he remembered all the tape. No. That couldn't be it. Kim wasn't just disappearing. Shane had to see him again. If nothing else he owed him a hell of a thank you.

"If you need more pain meds, you're supposed to push this." Braden showed Shane that taped to the hand with the IV and finger cuff there was a button near his only free digit, his thumb.

"I'm fine." The only thing bothering him was the twisting knot in his gut at the thought that Kim was gone.

"Braden?" Their mom was calling from somewhere past the curtains.

Braden stuffed his BlackBerry in his pocket with guilty speed. In a whisper he said, "I'll try and see if I can find him."

Braden's search took forever. Shane wished he could fall

asleep, but every time he started to drop off, he jerked awake to the nagging worry in his gut. Kim wouldn't just disappear without a goodbye. Without a *hey, here's my number, gimme a call and let me know how you're doin'*. Maybe he had a flight to catch. But he could have left a note.

Shane considered that for a second. Did Kim really seem like a guy to pen a nice-fuck, fun-saving-your-life, gotta-run note? He wouldn't have expected a postmortem from the guy he'd shoved his ass at on the boat, but the guy who'd been there with him for eight hours in open water, the guy who'd dragged him to shore and saved his fucking life? Yeah. He thought that at least warranted a "Glad you made it. Hell of a time."

His mom sat next to him with a pile of yarn on her lap. When he concentrated on it, he realized she was knitting something that looked flower-child gone chic for his soon-to-be niece or nephew. He couldn't remember her ever knitting before. Maybe it was a grandmother thing. It made her look...old. Or maybe that was on him. It couldn't have been easy dropping everything from her therapy practice and running down to Central America hoping her youngest son wouldn't die.

He rolled his head on the pillow for a better look, and all of the muscles in his neck and shoulders lit up with a pain that shot straight around his skull. What the fuck was that? Kim would know.

"Do you want a drink, honey?"

"Where's the doctor who came in with me?"

"Dr. Kim? I haven't seen him since yesterday." His mom knit a few more stitches, her brow doing the same. "What did you need? He seemed somewhat...severe."

"He saved my life." Shane knew he sounded defensive, but his mom had turned Kim's intensity into some kind of character flaw.

"I suppose if you were going to have that kind of a problem, it's good you did it with a doctor there."

Yes, Mom. We already know what a fuck-up I am. "Is he all right? Braden said he needed treatment when we came in."

"I imagine so. He's been fine every time I've seen him since we got here on Wednesday."

"How did you get here so fast?"

"I had Belize, dive tours and Sea Magic on Google alerts."

Wow. In his mom's mind, he was always going to be the five-year-old who broke his arm on his first trip to the playground with his brothers. He looked down at the hospital gown, the IV, the bandages on his hands. Maybe she wasn't far off.

His leg hurt, but not enough to really justify morphine. He was more inclined to punch that button so he could just drift away and not have to deal with any of the crappy feelings churning in his gut. But a drug addiction was a little extreme, even for him. In the eyes of his family, Shane was a fuck-up. And they all had twenty-twenty vision. Not exactly this-just-in, headline news.

He concentrated on the rhythmic whisper of yarn and the click of needles to try to lull himself somewhere he didn't have to deal with all the crap in his head.

It must have worked because when he opened his eyes, his leg hurt, his mom was gone and Kim and Braden were at the foot of his bed.

"I bought you about five mom-free minutes. Now I'm leaving before I see anything that scars me for life."

"Like what?" Shane asked.

"Dude, I saw enough of you when I had to change your

diapers. Your doctor can inspect you without me around."

Your doctor. Braden had always been the only one in the family with accurate gaydar. Their dad could trip over two guys fucking and think naked wrestling was a new Olympic sport.

"Bullshit. Mom did not make a seven-year-old change my diapers."

"That's what you think." Braden stepped behind Kim and struck a dramatic pose of hand on chest, head flung back. *A doctor*, he mouthed. *Try not to fuck it up*. He disappeared around the curtain.

Kim nodded in Braden's direction. "He's impressive."

"He's straight." Pain made him cranky. Kim leering at his brother pissed him the fuck off. Damn. This wasn't how he wanted this to go.

"So." Kim folded his arms and arched his brows. "You wanted to see me?"

"Uh yeah. No one seems to want to give me a straight answer. What happened to me?"

"You had a systemic reaction to the venom. Which is a medical way of saying your body freaked out and almost killed you. Your kidneys shut down. Your blood pressure dropped, possibly due to the hemolytic elements of the venom wreaking havoc on your red blood cells. Your spleen was enlarged."

Shane yanked the gown away from his chest. No lines of stitches; no surgery.

"Once the vitals were addressed—"

Vitals addressed. Meaning once Kim got Shane's heart back on line with some help from a few hundred joules.

"Thanks for that, by the way."

Kim nodded, one corner of his mouth curving. "After that it was a matter of getting fluids and an antihistamine into you. I had some concerns about rhabdomyolysis, and the lab reports aren't back yet, but I'd say as long as you avoid further envenomations, you will be fine."

"Is that your highly educated prognosis, 'fine'?"

Kim shrugged. "Life is always a crapshoot, Scuba Cowboy. I could tell you to stay out of the water, but I'd doubt it would take."

"I—I really owe you. You probably should have just left me in the water." Shane tried to find a way to make the words mean as much as they should, but sometimes even a good vocabulary was as useful as teats on a bull.

"It all worked out."

"Yeah." Aside from that *Scuba Cowboy*, the guy Shane had been fucking on the boat had disappeared behind this calm—and severe—doctor.

"The tour company put me up for a few days, sent over my belongings. I imagine they sent yours to your parents."

"Probably making nice so we don't sue. You know the captain didn't report us missing for hours."

"I heard." Kim looked at his watch. "My plane leaves in three hours. I'm sure your parents will have you on a plane home tomorrow."

Like Shane couldn't arrange his own transportation.

His empty stomach soured on acid. Nothing else for it to do since it was empty as a call-you-tomorrow promise issued to a bad one-night stand. What had Shane really thought would happen when he talked to Kim? Just because they'd been through a life-or-death experience together didn't mean they had some kind of bond. It was probably just another day at the office for Kim—with or without the mind-blowing sex as a prelude.

"You know, it didn't all suck. Some of it was fun."

"Except for the pain, the puking and the heart-stopping parts?"

"Yeah. Except for that. But I kind of think I'd do it all again—if I knew I was going to live."

Kim moved quickly, faster than Shane had ever seen him, yanking the curtain closed, sealing them in a mildew-scented cave. Without wasted motion, he leaned over Shane's bed and kissed him, sliding first hard then soft over Shane's cracked lips, one hand cupping the back of his head to lift him from the pillow. Despite a concern over how vile his breath probably was, it still felt nice. When Kim's hand tightened on his neck, it got a whole lot better than nice. And too damned short.

Kim lifted his head and then licked his lips. "I'm glad you did. If you're ever in Jacksonville, look me up."

For a second, Kim looked surprised, like he didn't mean to say it, but then he gave Shane one of those smiles, the kind he seemed to hoard to only give out to sunsets and when he thought of that guy Joey, and right now it was just for Shane, and if the drugs were making him so loopy that he wanted to write a fucking poem about that smile it was okay with him. Shane tried to grab Kim back, but the whole hands-strapped-down thing put a stop to it.

Kim stepped back, glancing at his damn watch. "Anything else?"

"Yeah." The kiss—even more that hand on his neck—had reminded him of a fact he'd managed to shove to the back of his mind for a few minutes. "I'd like this tube out of my dick and my hands free."

"I can free your hands, but you'd be better off having the nurse handle the catheter. They do hundreds."

"Don't want to give my dick a goodbye kiss?"

"Not under that context, no." Kim found a pair of surgical scissors in the cabinet next to Shane's bed and cut away the gauze and tape that had covered his hands like mittens. "There. You're free."

Shane wiggled his fingers. "Thanks again."

"Don't mention it." There was a dryness to Kim's tone that suggested a different meaning, but Shane's brain functions were too blurred by the morphine to figure it out.

Kim wadded up the bandages and put them on the table. "I really don't want to miss my plane. Take care of yourself, Scuba Cowboy."

By the next morning, Shane was ready to discharge himself. His parents had been dealing with the paperwork for more than two hours. Josh was on guard duty when Braden showed up with a guy in a suit that was way too nice for Belize City Memorial.

If Shane could peg the guy as an insurance company lawyer from a look, Mr. Corporate Law could probably name the firm and the guy's law school from the way he carried his briefcase. Josh stepped forward to block the suit's way. "No."

"Yes," Shane said. "Either I talk to him with you here or get waylaid sometime when you're not around."

"Smart little shit," Josh muttered.

The guy put his briefcase on the table next to Shane's bed. His skin was bronze, head shaved in deference to a dramatically receding hairline. "I guess you understand why I am here. I am Karl DeYonge." His accent was British, but tinged with more East than West Indies to Shane's ear. "I represent the interests of Sea Magic Dive Tours."

"Cut to the chase," Shane suggested.

"As I am sure you have deduced, I have been authorized to offer you a settlement."

"We're not interested," Josh said.

"Yes, we are. Are you telling me that it's better to wait ten years for it to settle and then lose most of the money to the courts and lawyers?"

"Your brother is right, Mr. McCormack."

"Which one?" Josh asked. He turned to Shane. "You know they're only going to offer you a fraction of what you could get in court."

"But a fraction right now."

DeYonge patted his briefcase. "I have a check ready for you, Mr. McCormack. Certified, of course."

"And what exactly would he be signing away?"

"There is a nondisclosure agreement, of course, and prohibition on further litigation. And Sea Magic Dive Tours assumes no blame for any pain or suffering Mr. McCormack might have experienced over the incident."

Incident. The captain left them to die, and then didn't call them in as missing. Shane knew the risks when he went into the water, but Kim...

"In exchange for?"

"A quarter of a million dollars."

Shane whistled.

Josh made a disgusted cough in his throat. "Because they know you could take them for ten times that at least. The book deal alone could net you two hundred thou. And you've got to think about—"

"Shut up, Josh. I'm not an idiot. What about my medical

expenses? What currency is that offer in?"

DeYonge's eyes glittered and then shadowed as he looked down. He could see his endgame now.

Shane didn't care. It wasn't about winning, it was about finishing this up and getting on with his life now that he still had one.

"The currency is naturally based on the adjudicating sovereignty—" DeYonge started.

And the Belizian dollar would devalue that by half. Shane looked steadily at DeYonge. "Here's the deal. Throw in medical coverage from the day the ship left the harbor until the end of this calendar year and put your offer in American currency and I'll sign off on it today."

Josh was going to damage his larynx if he kept coughing a growl like that. "You realize that if you have any other medical problems from this, you won't get coverage. Probably not even disability."

Shane nodded.

The lawyer cut in. "And you won't be able to discuss this settlement with anyone. Not just the press, but with the other party involved. That applies to you as his solicitor as well, Mr. McCormack."

"I understand," Shane said.

"Mr. McCormack?"

"I am familiar with the standard language, thank you," Josh snarled.

"I'll have to make a call to institute the changes. How much longer will you be in country?"

"Not long," Josh said. "And I'm going to try to get him to come to his senses."

"I'll try to have an offer for you today." DeYonge picked up his briefcase and left.

"You'd be an asshole to take that deal." Josh didn't even wait for DeYonge to clear the curtain.

"You've always thought I was anyway so what's the difference?"

"The difference is—Jesus—I don't want you to throw this away. It's a chance—"

"For what? Money I didn't earn? A chance to be rich and do nothing for the rest of my life?"

Josh met his stare and then threw up his hands, not in surrender but in disgust. "Fine. At least let me read the contract, okay?"

Shane nodded. Even if the offer got knocked down to two hundred thou, he could still write his own ticket anywhere. Even if the only place he could think of going at the moment was northeast Florida.

Chapter Ten

As a reward for his inadvertently extended vacation, Kim spent his first four days back in the hospital grabbing naps in the lounge and subsisting on swill from the cafeteria. Astonishingly, it was a quiet couple of days in trauma. One GSW, one arterial bleeder, and an accident with one DOA and one they lost in surgery. Of course all of those happened within twenty-four hours. The rest of the time he pulled in the ER: sprained ankles, strep throats, stitches and miscarriages.

At the end of the shift, he was making a break for fresh air when the head of trauma called him into his office.

Dr. Rewatiraman had a round blank face that hid a scalpel-sharp brain. He missed nothing that went on in his department, and respect for his skill was the number-one reason Kim had chosen Shands for his residency. Now all that acuity was focused on Kim and his decision about his fellowship.

"I won't say we wouldn't like to keep you here at Shands, but I'm afraid I cannot hold your slot indefinitely."

"I understand."

"Is there something tempering your decision?"

Nothing logical, and that was an alien sensation. Uncertainty was a potentially lethal trait in a surgeon. Still after the vacation he'd just survived, being stuck in Jacksonville and its proximity to Orlando was not as terrifying a prospect as it had been two weeks ago.

He bought himself five more days. "I'll have an answer for you next Monday. I'm still unpacking from my vacation."

"Very good." Rewatiraman leaned back in his chair. "I understand you did some fieldwork down there."

Shane's breath gone, pulse gone. Yes, it had been fieldwork. And the kind Kim never wanted to do again. In that instant, he knew why the night dives had been so unnerving. It was that black, cold void pulling on him in a way he'd almost managed to forget. Losing Shane's pulse on that too-long trip to a hospital brought back that fifteen-year-old moment when Kim had learned what dead really meant. No light. No answers. Just cold, permanent nothing.

And even when the paddles and the hypo brought back the flutter of life, Kim couldn't shake off that feeling like the emptiness was just waiting for another chance. It was there in every long space between the electric contractions of Shane's cardiac tissue. Nothing as sure as the knowledge that they were all nothing but animated meat just waiting for the power to go out.

Forcing back the thought, he schooled his voice to match the clinical analysis he had learned to deliver on rounds. "An unusual siphonophora envenomation. Complications resulting from a systemic reaction to the venom."

"I read the report. Good improvisation in the field. What would you have done in the event of anaphylaxis?"

"Repurposed gear or environmental elements into something to trache him." Trache Shane. Waiting for the helicopter, peeling back a lid and finding no trace of life behind a formerly bright blue eye.

"Exactly how long were you stranded out there?"

"I'm afraid I can't—"

"Right. Lawyers." Rewatiraman spat out the word with unprecedented emotion. "I will expect to hear from you on Monday then, Doctor."

Rewatiraman stood and offered his hand. Kim shook it and went home to sleep until his next shift.

The cab driver asked if he should wait, but Shane handed off the fare and tip with a shake of his head. Even if there had been a dozen Dr. Jae Sun Kims in Jacksonville, Shane knew he had the right place. The small house just looked like Kim. Nothing fussy, everything neat. But the kind of neat that came from habit, not aesthetics. Kind of antiseptic compared to some of the other places in the run-down neighborhood. Rows of small, one-story stucco houses that had all probably been white—or maybe flamingo pink like the one on the left—when someone plopped them here in the fifties.

He'd spent the night in a hotel even though he'd wanted to take a one-a.m. cab here right from the airport, had wanted to get out and push the plane a little faster, not so much because he couldn't wait to see Jay, but from the fear that with too much time to think about it, Shane would change his mind again. As the taxi turned at the end of the block, Shane hitched his duffle on his shoulder, frozen in indecision. What made him think Kim would be happy to see him?

Something about a kiss and a smile drifted around in the dopey haze of his hospital memories. With a clearer mind, he was less sure that he hadn't imagined it. His leg still burned, but he was off everything but Tylenol and vitamin E for his souvenir scars which looked like something out of a horror movie.

Ah fuck it. He was here now. He walked up to the front

door and pushed the bell. The Dr. Jae Sun Kim who yanked the wood away from Shane's knuckles before he could add a knock in case the bell was broken was his Jay all right, but a pissed-off, bed-headed, still-sexy-as-all-hell Jay. No shirt, bleach-spotted surgical scrub pants barely hanging on to the top of sharp hipbones. It wasn't like Shane hadn't seen it all before, but hell, it was worth more than a second look. As they stood there, Jay dragged a hand across his face, making it plain he'd just woken up. Shane knew the instant all the dots connected to make a picture in Jay's brain, because his face went completely blank.

Shane might as well have seen his air gauge read empty at the same second he realized he'd left his emergency tank on the boat.

Hell, he'd come all this way. Might as well push on through. "Hey."

Kim's face remained expressionless as he pulled the door open far enough for Shane to get inside and closed it behind him. Shane tried to hide the duffle behind his back.

"What are you doing here?" Kim's tone was as blank as his face.

"You said if I was in Jacksonville I should look you up, so I did."

"Why are you in Jacksonville?"

Yeah well, that was the sticky part of the question. Fucking bastard wasn't making it easy. Shane fell back on humor. "Haven't you ever heard of that custom where if you save someone's life you're responsible for them? Or maybe it's that they're responsible for you?"

Kim didn't move. Didn't even blink and Shane was kind of wondering if the guy's eyes were going to dry out from staring at him. He could use some back-up equipment right about now.

Finally, Kim folded his arms across his chest and raised his brows. There was his obnoxious, arrogant, make-Shane-crazy-enough-to-hop-on-a-plane-for-no-good-reason doctor.

"I find myself mercifully free of belief in any superstitions or customs."

"Fine, you son of a bitch. I came here to get fucked."

Shane couldn't tell exactly what it was, something in Kim's eyes, or maybe the set of his mouth, but in an instant his superior look shifted into something hot enough to melt a glacier, and Shane was so relieved he almost dropped the duffle and grabbed him then and there.

Kim pushed his hair out of his eyes. "I suppose I should be flattered that of all the cocks that would be willing to plow your tight ass you thought of mine."

"Yeah, well none of 'em come attached to an arrogant bastard who calls me baby."

The look on Kim's face made Shane wonder if maybe he'd gone a little too far that time, but then Kim pushed him back against the door, hand on the button of Shane's shorts, and going too far was all right if it got him done right.

"Careful, Cowboy." Kim's fingers dove into Shane's briefs, pulling up his balls and rubbing on the skin behind until Shane was trying to find some way to shift his hips to get more than just the occasional rub of Kim's wrist against the hard-on that was pushing its way out of Shane's shorts.

"Uh-huh." Kim gave him one, two nice tugs full of pressure, and Shane was as ready to go as he was ever going to be. "Could get yourself in trouble."

Shane let his head fall back against the door, heard a much louder thunk and realized it was his duffle hitting the floor. "What kind of trouble?"

"The kind..." a flick of his thumb over the head and then another, a rub in time with a long stroke up the shaft, and then back down, "...where..." slick with a little precome, Kim's thumb moved to rub behind Shane's balls, and back to put pressure on his hole, "...you don't get off."

Shane needed more. Tried to spread his legs, but he was pinned by his khakis, pinned by Kim.

"Thought that was kind of the point, Jay."

Kim pulled his hand free and stepped back. "Where you don't get off until I'm ready to let you."

Fuck if that didn't make him want to turn around and drop his shorts as much as it made him want to shove Kim onto his knees.

"And exactly how you think you're gonna manage that?"

Kim wrapped a hand around Shane's neck and pulled him down. Fuck if the bastard hadn't been right about Shane's wiring, because the weight of Kim's hand on that spot had Shane's knees starting to bend. He took a deep breath when he realized all Kim was pushing for was a kiss. Shane spread his legs until they were a little closer in height and met him halfway.

The answer whispered across Shane's lips. "Why don't you think about that for a minute?"

Shane started the kiss, but let Kim drive it. Hard pressure, no teeth, just the slick thrust of Kim's tongue. Shane got his fingers in Kim's hair, found it so soft and thick without the gel that a groan spilled from Shane's throat into Kim's.

Then the air tank ran empty. Shane couldn't find another breath as Kim slid to his knees with all the grace and control of a yoga instructor's wet dream. He wanted more strength in his neck to look down, but Kim's breath was hot and damp on his shorts, and oh fuck he was mouthing him through the cotton.

120

Shane started hoping the decorative woodwork on the door was up to him holding on to it while he got the most anticipated blowjob of his life.

Kim jerked the shorts open, let them drop to Shane's knees, and then all his dick got was the caress of Kim's breath, cheek and hair as he licked down the crease of Shane's hip, shoving his shirt up to leave a wet hot bite under his bellybutton.

Shane put a hand on Kim's head, and he flung it off. Shane got the message and went back to digging his nails into the wood. His fingers itched for another touch of that silky hair, but his dick was itching for so much more and that was the body part giving the orders. He couldn't exactly say Kim was teasing him. Exactly. But when Kim finally put that pretty mouth on Shane's dick, his world greyed out for a second because he felt like he'd been hanging on edge a whole lot longer than the bare minute Kim had been down there.

Shane didn't dare do any of the things he would normally do: rock in a little deeper, guide him with a hand, or even just relax and let his body do the talking, because he wouldn't risk anything that would stop that wet, sweet—hell, fucking perfect—pressure.

He even bit back a snort of laughter when he realized Kim had him as surely as if he'd put a rope around Shane's balls. Oh yeah. The son of a bitch knew exactly what he was doing.

He thought about rushing it, trying to force his body to the edge and let it go. See what the control freak did when Shane shot right the hell down that tight throat, but Shane had a feeling, no, he damned well *knew*, Kim wasn't going to let it get that far and Shane kind of wanted to see where this would take them.

Where it took them was into the living room, Shane cursing

as Kim pulled off just when the pressure built in Shane's balls. The second Shane stepped out of his shorts and briefs, Kim yanked off Shane's shirt and urged him onto a heavy cushioned chair, knees spread wide on the seat, arms folded across the back, eyes staring at the wall behind, the choreography so damned efficient Shane had to wonder how many other guys had willingly hopped up here to offer their ass. Kim even managed to avoid putting a hand on the knotted lines left from the sting as he pushed Shane's legs wide.

He didn't care how much practice Kim had, provided he used it right the hell now. Shane was afraid he might come to regret that "baby" crack. At this rate, he'd probably be able to get it up and come again three times before Kim would let him get off. The bastard had Shane by the short hairs, an equal grip on his curiosity and his horniness. The most potent combination Shane could think of.

And the ache of delayed orgasm pooling in his balls ought to have taught him a lesson, but Shane had been a wiseass a lot longer than he'd been having sex, and it was a hard habit to break.

"You do that like you've got a lot of practice arranging positions. You got a secret career as a porn director?"

Kim didn't answer. Shane swallowed back a throatful of nervous spit and rubbed his forehead on his arms. He was about to ask another question but he didn't. Kim's play now.

Movement behind him, barely a whisper of sound from his bare feet, but Shane felt the motion against his skin. He hated waiting like this, not being able to see what the hell was going on. Shane swore he'd almost chewed off his tongue trying to keep from making another smart remark, but damn it was worth it when Kim licked down Shane's spine.

Oh thank God he'd opted for a hotel and a shower. If he'd

been afraid to move with Kim's mouth on his dick, the flick of Kim's tongue on his ass paralyzed him. Another wet swipe and then Kim's thumbs dug in and held him wide.

Kim's breath licked across the tongue-wet skin. "Got anything else to say?"

Damn, Shane couldn't think of anything he wanted more than Kim eating his ass, but fuck if Shane was handing over both his balls for the privilege. He was keeping the left one. Just on principle. "Not a thing, *baby*."

Shane held his breath until Kim's chuckle vibrated against him. "Let's see if you say that again when your balls turn blue."

"Bring it on, Jay."

Oh fuck, did he bring it. Lips, tongue, wet and hot, and just when he couldn't stand the soft touch, needed something more, Kim used the edge of his teeth. Shane was damned sure every nerve in his body was setting off fireworks in Kim's honor. Shane's dick stood ready to carry a flag in the Kim parade.

When Kim slipped a finger in and licked around it, hard stretch and soft heat, Shane couldn't stop the motion of his hips as he rocked back for more. He knew it was going to happen a second before it did. The welted skin seemed to stick out an inch from his body—had even forced him into shorter shorts than he'd had on since he was four years old. He was already jumping out of the way when Kim's hand gripped tight around Shane's knee. Pain screeched out from the raw nerves, shoving away the sweet pleasure he'd been riding.

"Shit." Kim released him immediately. "Sorry."

"It's all right. Do it to myself in the shower. I think it's something I need to scrub off and then damn."

"I'll get you some hydrocortisone cream or a—"

"Hey, Jay, I came to see you, not Dr. Kim." The pain might

have taken the edge off Shane's hard-on, but now that the worst of the electric shock had faded, he really wanted to get back to where they left off because Kim was as good with his mouth as he was with his hands and his dick.

Kim ran soothing hands up Shane's back, thumbs a good deep pressure in the muscles along his spine. "Actually, I think you said you came here to get fucked."

"I did. You wanna maybe get on that?"

"I do." But Kim's hands were frustratingly gentle as he pulled Shane back, angling his ass lower.

"You need a stepstool or something, Jay?"

One finger-full of lube, the whisper of latex and Kim shoved his way inside, stretching Shane hard and fast. "I don't know. You tell me."

At least Shane had the satisfaction of hearing Kim grunt between his words. Shane shifted his hips, trying to get over the whole ow-ow-too-fast and into something good. It wasn't like they were doing this regularly. Before they'd met he figured he'd gotten fucked maybe three times in five years.

"I think you're good," he managed as the burn eased. Now he wanted motion, but he wasn't giving Kim the satisfaction of asking for it. The bastard was already too damned cocky.

Kim laughed and dragged his cock back until the widest part of him was tugging on the tightest part of Shane, popped the rim in and out and then slammed deep.

"You think?"

Ah fuck. "Yeah. You're good."

God, better than good, but Shane was hanging on to that last bit of information until he needed it. He gripped the top of the chair and fucked back, tightening his ass on the thick cock inside him until they both grunted.

Kim pounded forward stroke after stroke, and Shane settled in for a hard, fast fuck, the quick and dirty flood of heat already coiling in his guts. Then Kim pushed down on Shane's lower back and slowed to a steady drag that circled over his gland, over nerves aching with the stretch, over everything that was good and right in the world.

Damn. Fucking someone with experience and knowledge was worth the sting, the crummy Belize hospital and the interminable plane ride next to a chatty middle-aged woman with seventeen hundred pictures to share from her iPhone. Hell, it was even worth putting up with Kim's shitty social skills.

The pressure inside pulsed sparks into Shane's dick, and he tightened his muscles again. He didn't know what he was trying to do. Keep the pressure steady, make it harder, more intense or just get Kim so crazy he'd fuck him till they got off so they could do it again. Kim rubbed his cock back and forth, burying himself deep and making tiny jerks with his hips, each one making Shane gasp. Jesus, he needed more friction, needed something before he was the one going crazy. Kim had better be kidding about that whole not-letting-him-come thing. How was he going to stop Shane anyway?

Shane found out when he reached down to fist his cock.

Kim grabbed his shoulder and started pounding so hard and fast, Shane had to slam both his hands into the wall above his head before he got fucked clean through it. With every thrust Kim used that leverage to drag Shane down before driving him into the wall again. Shane wasn't thinking about coming or not coming, just about how strong Kim was and how good it felt to get fucked like this.

Shane groaned again because he wanted to let him know, and words weren't going to happen, he groaned every time that thick cock forced him wide as it pulled out, desperate for the next push that would fill him. When Kim reached up and yanked on his hair, Shane was ready to gift-wrap his balls for Kim because principles didn't make nice with sex like this.

Shane had no idea he'd get off by being so well and truly fucked by such an arrogant little SOB. Another hard tug on his hair and the arrogant little SOB had Shane's neck stretched tight for a kiss and a suck on the skin. Christ, he could feel him everywhere. The wet heat of Kim's mouth spread all the way down Shane's spine.

One more deep thrust and Kim stopped.

They'd only fucked a few times, and Kim was quiet, but not that quiet.

"Did you come?" Shane couldn't help feeling a little bit of triumph after all Kim's talk of making Shane wait.

"No."

Shane waited. It wasn't easy, but since doing what Kim had in mind had so far led to incredible sex, Shane was working on the patience thing.

"I want to switch..."

Shane's brain jumped ahead of Kim's words. Oh yeah. Switching would be fine. And Shane wouldn't give a shit if his thigh burned when it was slamming against Kim's hip.

"...positions."

And Kim's words finally caught up with Shane's brain.

"Oh. Okay."

Kim pulled out and Shane absolutely did not collapse onto the chair, and it wasn't just because of Kim's arm around Shane's waist, pulling him to stand on his shaking legs. The bastard had endurance, Shane had to give him that.

Kim edged around and sat in the chair, and Shane already liked this idea. He'd get to watch. The chair didn't have arms

126

and Shane could brace his feet on the floor when he sat on Kim's dick. The chair was so perfect for this, Shane had to wonder if that's why Kim had bought it.

Shane straddled him easily enough, reaching behind to meet Kim's hand as they both guided his cock back inside. Even better now, no burn, just getting everything that had been aching and empty rubbed right again. Shane could hold Kim's shoulders and let him push his hips up. Shane wouldn't have to work for it at all.

He should have known Kim couldn't just let it be that easy. He grabbed on, hand on Shane's hip and the other slung around his neck to drag him into a kiss, Kim's tongue working Shane's mouth like the cock worked his ass. The ridges of Kim's abs dragged against Shane's dick like an awkward-angle hand job.

Kim was gasping now, though Shane had to wonder if it was from just the kiss. Kim had everything mapped out to the point where Shane felt like his presence here mattered less than the furniture Kim was fucking him on. Sex should be messy and impulsive, and even when it was anonymous, at least for those few minutes you ought to be aware of who was sucking your dick. Not this careful arrangement of everything set up so there wasn't a false move, no slips or laughs.

But it was hard to bitch about it when it felt so fucking good. Kim's hands moved down to Shane's ass, pulling and stretching, more sensation, tight stretch, thick friction. Kim pressed a finger over the skin already taut as a balloon stretched to popping. If he did that thing where he rubbed under Shane's balls at the same time...

Of course Kim did. He was the perfect fucking partner, everything calculated to the inch to show off how goddamned good he was. But knowing that didn't stop Shane's body from shuddering, from him fucking himself on those waves of sensation, from letting Kim work him, ass and mouth and cock, from loving everything Kim wanted Shane to feel.

When the ache of needing to come hurt like he was fighting for air to breathe, he didn't have to beg. Kim was the one who dragged Shane's hand to his cock, guided him until Shane's brain connected enough to find the rhythm, jacking himself in time with the way Kim's hips drove him up, hitting deep and sharp inside. With a hand on his neck, Kim pulled him down into another wet kiss.

Shane wasn't sure he could go with that much pressure filling him, that much feeling overloading his nerves. Kim let go of his neck, and Shane arched up, the angle taking Kim deeper, and it was right fucking there.

Shane's hand sped up without him telling it to and first it was just a sweet spark, like scratching the itch of morning wood in the shower, and it was good, but kind of disappointing if after all that a little ripple of release was all he was going to get.

"Shane."

His eyes popped open. Jay's face, flushed dark. Lips shining around his open mouth, eyes softer than Shane had ever seen them. That little sweet spark touched off a cartoon line of gunpowder right up Shane's spine and back down, setting off an explosion that rushed from his balls to his dick, hitting his bloodstream like a pure sugar rush, and he fought to keep his eyes open to watch his cock jet thick white ropes, one of them landing at the corner of Jay's pretty mouth. He flicked it with his tongue, drew it in and smiled. Shane couldn't keep his eyes open anymore as the hard spasms ripped him inside out.

Kim kept pounding him, like he wouldn't stop until Shane had spilled some of his soul right along with his spunk. His ass burned, but he just hung on, hands splayed out on Kim's chest, and watched his dark eyes squeeze shut as he grunted and shook and came for a nice good while, dick jerking inside Shane.

Dropping his head down like a spent horse, Shane worked on getting back some oxygen. He tried to think of the last time he'd been light-headed after sex and came up with a never. Kim's hands soothed his back, gliding on sweat-soaked muscles. It would have felt nice but for the buzz of resentment that had Shane feeling like he was being petted and patronized. He got enough of that from his own family. He didn't need it from a boyfr—Kim.

As usual, his pride was no match for his hedonism and he lay there, enjoying every long stroke of Kim's hand.

"You're not going to hyperventilate again, are you?"

Shane jerked his head up. "No." He didn't need the sarcasm any more than he needed soothing. He needed a shower. And a plane trip somewhere besides this micro-managed—his cock twitched with an aftershock—dick heaven.

Kim rubbed the back of Shane's neck. The plane and Shane's pride were going to have to wait until he had some strength back in his legs.

Kim's sigh cooled the sweat on Shane's neck. "I'm starving. Want some pizza?"

Shane lifted his head. "It's ten thirty in the morning."

"I know a place that delivers twenty-four hours."

"Of course you do."

"Pepperoni and meatballs all right?"

Shane could pick off the pepperoni. "If we can have extra cheese."

Chapter Eleven

Kim jerked awake with the usual burst of adrenaline. Since his residency, he hadn't slept more than three contiguous hours without an abrupt slam into consciousness, brain racing to solve whatever crisis was forming in the ER. But he wasn't at the hospital. He was home. In his full-sized bed, which was infinitely less roomy with a full-sized Scuba Cowboy in it. A Scuba Cowboy who hogged not only the mattress but Kim's pillow and breathed weird snuffling noises into Kim's ear. It wasn't a snore, more like a rumbling chuckle, like Shane's dream was funny.

Kim had bizarre dreams and terrifying dreams and arousing dreams, but he couldn't remember any funny dreams. He could count on his...nose the number of men who had slept the night with him in his bed. It was the same number of men who had sat on his couch with an artery-hardening amount of cheese dripping from a lickable chin, who grabbed the remote and flipped rapidly through television channels Kim didn't even know he got.

Finally Shane had left it on the repeat of some asinine medical drama long enough for Kim to start pointing out at least fifteen inaccuracies in five minutes while Shane laughed and scooped up the last congealing slice off the cardboard.

They had fallen asleep on the couch with some sort of

sports program droning in the background, Kim's legs hooked around Shane's where they flopped on the coffee table. Kim's built-in timer didn't have time to go off, because Shane woke Kim up by waving a plate of fluffy scrambled eggs and—were those biscuits?—under his nose. Jesus. He'd need to start a course of statins after today to counteract the effect on his arteries.

"You cook?" he asked.

"Well, I can make eggs."

"And biscuits." Despite his better judgment, Kim grabbed one and bit into flaky, sweet, buttery goodness. "I didn't even know I possessed the necessary ingredients."

"You didn't, exactly. But I can wing it. I like to eat."

Now after replaying that afternoon conversation in his head, Kim turned on his side and took advantage of Shane's lack of consciousness to make a slow inspection. As much as he might like to eat, the hard lines of Shane's body were clearly visible in the blue glow from the digital clock. He probably had one of those annoying metabolisms where he could eat a box of donuts and do nothing but fuck and sleep and never gain an ounce. Yoga did not provide sufficient cardio work to keep a body like Shane's.

Despite the a/c, the midnight air was sticky with humidity, but when Kim brushed his hand across Shane's shoulder, trying to push for a little more mattress space, the skin was as cool and dry as fresh sheets. If he was going to hog the bed, Kim would just sleep on top of him.

Shane's eyes opened. "Sorry. Was I snoring?"

"No."

Shane leaned up on an elbow and ran a hand through his hair, squeezing his scalp as if trying to wake himself up. The sheer size of him, the gesture that had somehow become familiar in only a few days, tugged on Kim's balls like a slow flicking tongue. Now Kim's brain wasn't the only thing awake and ready.

"Do you know what else you aren't doing?"

"What's that?" Shane dropped his hand and sat up, a wariness around his eyes that made Kim think of the Shane Kim had seen after the sting, Shane without his cocky assurance and in-your-face twang. Maybe Shane thought the answer to that question was *You aren't sleeping here.* And it was a question Kim was going to ask in the morning. Exactly how long did Shane plan on hanging around when his stated purpose had been to come get fucked?

"You aren't blowing me."

Shane's grin flashed, bright in the dark room. "Now how did I miss that little detail?"

Kim arched his brows.

"Well, maybe not so little."

Kim cuffed the side of Shane's big shaggy head. And Shane laughed, leaning over to lick at Kim's jaw. He must have liked the taste of the sweat Kim could feel drying on his skin because Shane buried his face in Kim's neck with a deep groan, his thick hair tickling the side of Kim's face.

Kim moved his thigh and discovered that Shane was clearly interested in the suggestion. Shane ground down and shifted his hips until their cocks lined up. Frottage was nice, but it wasn't what Kim had had in mind. The grinning face above him reminded him that with their time on the boat cut short, Kim hadn't found a chance to fuck that mouth like he'd been planning.

"Now why doesn't this feel like a blowjob?"

"It will. Gonna come on you, Jay. And then I'm going to lick it off you, eat it right off your dick."

Kim's hips bucked up. The idea was hot, but he couldn't let go of the idea of Shane straddling him, bobbing on his cock while Kim worked a thumb into Shane's ass and felt the reaction echo from his ass to his mouth to Kim's dick.

He put his hands up on the broad chest acting like a low-hanging ceiling and tried to steer him lower.

Shane slowed his grind and tipped his head down in Kim's range of vision. "Got a problem with that?"

Not exactly. But Shane had been willing to go along with every other suggestion Kim had made with words or movements. Maybe Kim wasn't done scaling this particular mountain.

Still. He wanted to know. "You liked it."

"Huh?"

"You like it when I take charge."

"Hell yeah, I do. But that don't mean I don't like to change things up. I'm not some blow-up doll to fuck and put in the closet, Jay."

"You run your mouth far too much for me to ever think that."

"Thought you liked my mouth." Shane licked his lips.

"I do. And that's what I had in mind at the start of this."

"This?" Shane showed off his pushup skills by lifting his hips up while resting on his elbows. "This is called sex, Jay. And you just do what feels good. You don't plan out every last bit of it."

Kim had another answer for that. Something along the lines of talking and not doing was no better than planning it out. But Shane lowered himself back down and sealed Kim's words and the gasp that resulted from the renewed friction with a kiss. The sleep-stale taste of their mouths disappeared after a few licks of Shane's tongue, or maybe it got lost in the distracting pressure of Shane's dick, his chest, his hands alongside Kim's face.

A quick suck and Kim's tongue slipped into Shane's mouth with a tug that went right to Kim's dick just as Shane worked the roots of their cocks together. Heat ripped low and deep inside Kim's belly. Fuck plans. Fuck everything. Kim rolled Shane onto his side. Want flashed hotter with the spark of anger when he felt Shane's smile against his lips.

Kim pushed Shane's head down. "Suck me."

Plan or no plan, that smiling supercilious mouth was going around his cock, and Kim was going to fuck his way deep into Shane's throat until he stole his breath—the breath they'd both fought so hard for on that scrap of land—with his dick, because he wanted it. No, he needed it. Needed Shane to yield, to swallow him down and let Kim ram his cock past his lips.

Shane groaned as he licked his way down Kim's sternum. A couple sloppy swipes of tongue on Kim's dick and Shane's lips pressed against the tip.

"Let me in."

Shane opened his mouth and Kim pushed in until he felt the soft heat of Shane's throat on the head of his cock.

Shane moaned again and pressed his tongue hard against the underside.

"Open up." Kim tugged hard on Shane's hair and felt his throat move, swallow Kim deeper, tight muscles rippling on his cock. Shane grabbed him by the hips and rolled, so that Kim was on top, and he hadn't been wrong, his cowboy liked it like this. Liked turning over the reins and getting done. Kim pushed up so that he was sitting, straddling Shane's face, stroking his cheeks with a thumb to feel them rub against Kim's dick sliding in and out as he fucked Shane's mouth.

This was better than any answer Kim could have given the wiseass: his dick buried in Shane's throat. A perfect answer until Shane's eyes opened and he winked. Still so goddamned cocky. Kim used his calves to pin Shane's arms and put his hands behind Shane's skull to lift him by the back of the neck to make the angle better, let Kim work deeper into Shane's throat. Shane's eyes drifted closed again and he sucked, hummed and groaned around Kim's dick.

Kim shuddered, listening to Shane's breaths thicken to gasps. Everything wetter, messier now that Shane couldn't swallow. Jesus. Kim had never done anything like this before. Never dived in for just himself and fuck if the other guy got off. Words rolled through his brain and he kept them safely locked behind his lips. *Take it, baby. So good. God, so fucking good.*

His fingers brushed Shane's cheeks again, found them slick with more than spit. It took a full second for Kim's brain to catch up and recognize that specific sensation of moisture. He wiped another tear from the corner of Shane's eye.

"Jesus." Kim had lost his fucking mind. Because of a wink?

He eased back, but Shane lifted his head and followed, freeing an arm and pulling Kim's hips forward again. A tiny shake of Shane's head tore away the last bit of decency Kim had been clinging to. He bucked with his hips, again and again, and Shane's free hand snaked around Kim's hips, pressing on the spot behind his balls and triggering a minor nuclear event at the base of Kim's spine. Heat rushed from his balls to his cock, poured through him like radioactive isotopes until even Shane's mouth was cool against the burning skin of Kim's dick.

He came back from the land of conscience-free orgasms to find Shane looking up at him with wet eyes, a swollen mouth and a come-splattered face. Shane rubbed circles on Kim's hipbones with rough thumbs as another shudder echoed through him.

"Damn. You really are a control freak." But Shane grinned when he said it, then winced, bringing a hand to his face. "My jaw is fucking killing me."

A control freak. Kim had never been more out of control in his life. He had rutted, fucked Shane's mouth until he was gagging for breath, and he almost hadn't been able to pull back. Almost didn't care when he felt that tear on his finger. "Sorry."

"Don't be." Shane bucked a little and Kim swung off him. "Almost came from fucking nothing but air."

Kim wasn't sure he could summon either the enthusiasm or the coordination for even a hand job. "What do you—?"

"Roll over."

Kim's gut tightened, but he did as Shane's hoarse voice asked. Kim's behavior was the reason Shane sounded like that, so he supposed—

"Relax. Ain't gonna fuck you. Just gonna rub on your ass. Keep it tight, yeah?"

Shane's dick settled into the crease of Kim's ass, weight settling down, body warm and slick with sweat. It felt good, like a sauna after a hard workout, heat pooling in acidic muscles.

Shane opened his mouth and moved it soft and wet and full of moans against Kim's shoulder. Shane's dick slid along the crease, a not-unpleasant pressure when the root of Shane's cock hit Kim's asshole, nothing like penetration. He dragged a last bit of energy to himself and tightened the muscles to give Shane more friction.

"Damn. Yeah. Like—" Shane groaned into Kim's clavicle until the vibrations traveled deep to the marrow. A few quick jerks and Shane went still as he spat slick warmth onto Kim's back.

Kim barely had time to think of how uncomfortable the sticky cooling mess would be when sleep hit him like an ampoule full of anesthesia, Shane still draped on him like a grizzly bearskin rug.

Sometime in the next hour or two Shane moved off, leaving the dead weight of his legs on Kim's as Shane twisted at the hips to flop on the one clean spot on the sheet. Kim was still summoning up the energy to shove him off the rest of the way when he realized he hadn't woken to his internal clock but to the persistent peal of his front door bell.

He found his discarded scrubs between the living room and bedroom and hauled them up as he headed for the door. The pealing changed to a banging fist, and Kim was afraid he knew what he'd find when he yanked it open.

Sometimes he hated to be right.

Two familiar faces at the door, neither of them as welcome as his visitor yesterday. Kim sighed. Joey. And worse, Aaron.

"Jesus Christ." There was no way out of this without extensive humiliation. And Shane wondered why Kim preferred dead or anesthetized people for company.

"Good morning to you too," Aaron said with a suspicious wrinkle of his nose.

Shit. Kim probably reeked of come. If Shane just slept on, Kim could give them coffee and a quick story and—Aaron's eyes were looking past him into the living room.

Kim turned. Shane in nothing but those too-small khaki shorts, rubbing at his stomach and probably sending flakes of dried semen onto the carpet.

"Hey. Ya got company. Sorry. I'm a—" His drawl had never

sounded so thick or his voice so husky.

Kim surprised himself with the flash of triumph from wondering if it was the fact that his dick had been so far down Shane's throat two hours ago. "This is Shane. We met in Belize."

As the introduction prodded Shane forward, Kim was thrilled to see that Shane was two inches taller than that arrogant prick Aaron.

"Hmph." Aaron tilted his head and made that cough-laugh-growl thing that irritated everyone who had the misfortune to meet him. He looked back to Kim. "I thought I told you not to bring home any tacky souvenirs."

Chapter Twelve

Dr. I-Hate-People Kim turned out to have some friends after all, though Shane wasn't sure they were friends like the way he understood the word to work. The taller one engaged in a constant battle of one-upmanship like any good ol' boy hanging around a pickup drinking canned beer. And the other one, the blond with the bubble butt and the too-tight T-shirt that read "I Taught Your Boyfriend That Thing You Like" acted like he expected every guy in the vicinity to fall in love with his hot ass.

Shane might be a fuck-up but his mother had tried to raise him right, so he followed the cues from his host—cues that were all about keeping the guests out of the living room and herding them onto the screened-in porch, or the lanai as Jay called it. As they settled onto some uncomfortable plastic chairs, Shane wondered if the reason Kim was so intent on keeping them out here was because he was afraid that the living room might smell a bit like the back room of one of San Antonio's more liberal drinking establishments. Being pretty ripe himself made it hard to tell. He tried to keep downwind, but if people didn't call before dropping in, they had to take what they could get.

The blond watched Shane with a considerable amount of interest, eyes as wide as a cartoon character's. He found that putatively innocent scrutiny more annoying than the obvious condescension from the man who had called him a tacky souvenir.

Damn. Hadn't Jay ever had a...date before? Shane laid the drawl on as thick as cicadas on an oak tree in July. Working on the dive tour had given him plenty of practice in breaking the ice. He started with, "So how do y'all know each other?"

The tall man rolled his eyes. "I think a better question is why the fuck isn't there any coffee?"

"You know where the kitchen is," Kim said.

"He had a vat of it at home and we stopped at a Starbucks," the blond said.

"You're drinking Starbucks now?" Kim's tone implied a deep moral character flaw in the action.

"I get it where I can like any good addict." The tall man turned to face Shane. "Guess Kim's displaying his usual shitastic social skills. Aaron Chase." He didn't hold out a hand, so Shane just nodded.

"I'm Joey." The blond extended a hand.

Of course. Joey, fucking Joey, the guy who could put that smile on Kim's face, had turned his head to stare at the ugly mess all over Shane's knee.

"Holy shit," Joey breathed, garnering the attention of his prick of a boyfriend.

"What the fuck is that?" Aaron said. "You guys doing some kinky shit?"

"It's a long story," Kim answered.

"Let's go, Joey. I am not listening to Dr. Kim's Perverted Bedtime Stories."

Joey didn't say a word, he just looked at Aaron. They had some sort of silent communication, and then Aaron said, "All right. But I'm really going to need more coffee."

"All I have is hazelnut." Kim was lying.

Shane had been all through those cupboards looking for some baking powder yesterday. There were three kinds of fine artesian roasts in there, and none of them were messed up with a flavor like hazelnut.

"The fuck you do." If Aaron was what passed for a friend, Shane was starting to see why the doctor didn't spend much time with non-patient-type humans.

Kim merely flipped Aaron off.

Joey stared at the welts on Shane's leg. "We're so sorry to drop in like this. I knew he was back, but then Aaron said he had a really long shift at the hospital and he needed a day of sleep, but I couldn't wait anymore. There was some kind of accident, right?" He bent down for a closer look.

Hell if Shane was going to avoid talking about what had happened out there with Kim—or as that lawyer had put it—the other party involved. They could take the money back before he'd give that up. But he wasn't about to get into it with strangers, especially not these two, when Shane couldn't decide if they actually gave a shit about Kim or were the kind who fed off other people's misery.

"Careful. What if it's catching?" Aaron said.

Without even looking at the other man, Joey tossed off a "Don't be such a prick." His eyes suddenly widened. "Holy shit. Man-o'-war?"

Shane nodded.

"Crap. That must have hurt. I've never seen anyone with this bad a sting."

Before Shane could ask exactly how much experience Joey had with marine life, Joey said, "I surf. I've seen a couple guys get stung before, but usually they're lucky enough with the wet suit."

Lucky. That wasn't a word often applied to Shane. "I wasn't wearing a full one."

"I guess not. Aaron is a paramedic."

Shane wasn't sure if Joey's statement was an explanation for Aaron's asshatted behavior or had some kind of connection to the sting marks. Then it hit Shane that Joey was finally answering the question Shane had posed a good ten minutes ago.

Joey went on. "He knows Jae Sun from the hospital."

So Joey got to call him Jae Sun?

"Jay's a hell of a doctor," Shane said.

"Shane had a systemic reaction to the stings. We were stranded on a reef while we waited for help," Kim explained.

"So, *Dr.* Kim." Aaron used the title like an insult. "How'd you like fieldwork, away from all your fancy machines? Maybe now you could cut us paramedics a little slack when we bring 'em in and you don't like the way we hooked up the IV."

Kim leveled a look at Aaron. "Yes. I will."

Aaron sat back in his chair. "Well fuck. You guys must have had a hell of a time down there."

Shane felt like he owed Kim a little defense from this asshole Aaron, non-disclosure clause registering as non-important in the face of what Shane owed the guy sitting in that cheap plastic chair next to him. "Kim saved my life. We were out there with nothing for hours. He figured out a way to keep me breathing. If it weren't for him, my parents would be picking out my coffin."

Aaron studied Shane for a minute. "Does the melodrama come naturally with the hair or the accent?"

"You can see why they're friends," Joey explained. "They like to have this pissing contest over who's a bigger prick."

"Well, if it's over who *has* a bigger prick—" Aaron began.

"It's got to be Jay," Shane finished. "I'm still bowlegged after last night."

"I thought that was your natural condition, Tex," Aaron said.

"Not until we hooked up." Helping Jay out with this little pissing contest was the least he could do. 'Sides, it was probably true.

For a second, Shane thought he'd gone too far again. Kim's brows came together and then he laughed. Full, undignified, snorts-from-his-nose laughter.

He wiped away snot on the back of his hand. "Chase, you—
"

Shane had seen Kim laugh a bit, but never to the point where he couldn't form words. "I think the word you're looking for there is *owned*, Jay."

"Fucking mountain climber," Aaron said.

"Thank you." Jay gave Aaron a mock salute.

"And thanks a lot for the help, Joey," Aaron muttered.

"Like you need it." Joey wrapped his arms around Aaron's neck. "I thought everyone in Jacksonville had already seen it." He looked up and blinked those wide brown eyes. "He's totally hung. Feel better?" Joey smacked the top of Aaron's head.

"Now I won't fuck you." But Aaron's hand had come up to capture Joey's hand, and he toyed with his fingers in a way that made Shane almost blush.

"Yeah, I live in terror of that threat daily." Joey dropped on Aaron's lap. The plastic chair groaned against the cement.

"And still there's no coffee," Aaron complained.

Kim didn't seem inclined to bother and Shane could scarcely blame him, but Joey jumped to his feet and headed for the kitchen door like he owned the damned place. A force of nature, Jay had called him. And Shane was...Cheetos. What the fuck was he doing here?

"Hey, Shane." Joey stopped at the screen door. "Want to give me a hand?"

Shane didn't see what kind of help Joey needed, but at least he could show Aaron that the accent and the hair came with better manners than whatever passed for them with these two around.

When he got in the kitchen, Joey just poured himself a glass of juice and leaned back against the counter. "It's funny."

Shane was getting a bit extra-pissed now. He didn't usually take a dislike to someone, but he thought he might be willing to make an exception. "What's funny?"

"You don't like me."

"Hell, man, I just met you. I don't even know you." Shane banged through cabinets again, finding the filter and the coffee.

"And what's funny," Joey said as if Shane hadn't spoken, "is that people usually do." There wasn't any arrogance in Joey's statement. It was completely matter-of-fact. "Are you jealous? Because you don't have to be. Jae Sun has never been interested in me like that."

"I've got no reason to be even if he was fucking you six ways from Sunday."

"Really? That's why you followed him from Belize? Because you don't care where he puts his dick?"

Shane thought about that for a second. It didn't have as much to do with where Jay put his dick, but with how his face lit up when he thought about Joey.

"What, you and Aaron don't fuck around?"

"We've got all we can handle at the moment. But it wouldn't

be just about another cock that would set me off."

At least Joey was acting like Shane was smart enough to figure out what Joey wasn't saying.

"I only met Jay a week ago."

"I fell in love with Aaron from the minute we met—well, from the first time we fucked for sure." Joey grinned.

Shane almost answered the smile with one of his own, but he wasn't ready to give in yet. "I'm not saying—I like the guy, I do—but I just tend to—"

"Drift?"

God, Shane got enough of that from his mother and his sister. "What are you, some kind of therapist?"

"Yep. Though I work—if you can believe it—as a consultant for the police department. You're the youngest of three, maybe five. And by more than four years, I bet."

"You do this psychic act for the cops?" Shane shoved the carafe under the faucet and filled it. The immature part of Shane, the part that was the surprise baby of four, the whoops-mom-you're-not-done baby, wanted to dump it over Joey's head. It wasn't as if Shane didn't know all the psychological reasons for him being the fuck-up he was, though he liked to think bad luck had something to do with the depth of some of the crap he found himself in, he just didn't see anything needing to change.

Joey finished his juice and rinsed out the glass. Without having to search like Shane had done, the blond went right to the cabinet that held the dishes and got out four mugs. "I don't care if you like me. But Jae Sun is my friend. I'm not claiming I know him really well. He can be hard to read. But the fact that you're here—still here—when no one else has been says a lot."

Shane took that in. He'd been guessing that Jay was too

busy for boyfriends while he was doing all that work to be a doctor, but he sure wasn't too busy to practice fucking. Not based on Shane's experience.

Joey went on, "Jae Sun's got pretty good defense mechanisms, even better than Aaron—but don't tell either of them I said so. So what I wanted to tell you was this. Don't even think of cutting through all Jae Sun uses to keep himself safe and then pull that drifting shit."

"What are you, the gay mafia? I'll find myself in stylish cement shoes if I do?"

Joey shrugged.

"You're right. I don't like you. But I do like Jay. And that's all the explaining I'm going to do."

Joey looked at him, something Shane couldn't quite figure out in that steady brown gaze. Then he nodded and pulled out the sugar.

"Don't tell me your big, bad boyfriend needs sugar."

"I thought you'd like some."

Now exactly how the fucking hell could Joey figure on Shane's sweet tooth just from a five-minute conversation, during which he hadn't put anything in his mouth. Flustered, he said, "So, guess you spend a lot of time here?"

Joey grinned. "Maybe once a month. Aaron and I get into these knock-down drag outs and I need a place to cool down. I always swear I'm not going to let him push my buttons, but he does." Joey's eyes got bigger. "Oh, I sleep on the futon though. The one in the spare room."

Was that supposed to be an example of a healthy relationship? Shane couldn't imagine getting that worked up over something, and if he did, he sure as hell wouldn't be going back the next day.

"Why don't y'all just break up?"

Joey looked at him like Shane was a two-headed calf. "Because it's just a fight. Haven't you ever heard couples fight?"

Shane had, but he usually tried to get as far away from the sound as possible. His mom and Megan had tempers. When their husbands pissed them off, it got scary. And Josh was no slouch in the nasty-remarks department. Shane didn't get why anyone wanted to stick around to keep doing that.

"You'll get it after you have your first fight," Joey said with the kind of patronizing—well technically matronizing—wisdom Shane was used to getting from his mother.

Trying to follow Joey's chatter was like trying to track a ricocheting bullet. "Get what?" Shane asked.

"A lot. And don't try to pull that dumb-hick act with me. You're as smart as hell or Jae Sun wouldn't have looked twice." Joey got a paper towel and wiped up a spot where the water had dripped. "After you fight, you'll know. Even if you don't know now."

"Know what?" Shane wasn't acting. He knew, but somehow it might be easier if Joey said it. Someone ought to say it, and Shane couldn't see either him or Kim busting out with the words anytime soon.

Joey gave him that two-headed calf look again as he stepped toward the garbage pail. Then he stopped, cocked his head and made a shushing motion with his finger.

Shane just stared back. Joey rolled his eyes and waved Shane closer to the window over the sink. The sill was high, and Joey was leaning over the sink to peer out of it. Shane managed to ignore that distracting ass and put his attention to the window.

He couldn't see anything but Kim and Aaron talking on the lanai.

"And then the ambulance took him to the hospital and that's it," Kim was saying.

"So how the fuck did he end up here?"

Oh. Joey wanted to eavesdrop. It was childish and stupid. And fuck if Shane didn't want to hear Kim's answer to Aaron's question.

"Ask him," was all Kim said.

"I think you'd better do some asking."

"Chase, this is not like you and your little dick magnet. I don't take in strays and get all attached to them."

Shane pointed at Joey and mouthed, "You?"

Joey just smiled.

"I didn't take him in, he just wouldn't go." Aaron's voice was close to a growl.

"Right. And the kids? They keep coming home. And the nephew? And the dog? Face it. If you were any more maternal, you'd grow tits."

Shane had to cover his mouth. Jay could definitely bring it.

"So you're just going to let him take up space because he makes your dick happy and that's going to be it, right?"

"Last time I checked getting that sort of home delivery was expensive and risky. Tell me you don't like the convenience."

Calling them assholes was an insult to—assholes. Shane had probably had worse conversations about guys he had fucked, but he hadn't done it in front of someone's boyfriend. He glanced over at Joey, but he just looked as amused as he had at the dick magnet and stray comments.

Aaron's chair scraped the floor, and he spoke so low that Shane could only catch the end of it. "...more than that. It's not just the sex."

"If that's what you want to think. But you and I have both been there at the end enough times to know that there's nothing left when the electricity goes out, and all the shit people tell themselves won't change it."

"You're really a ray of sunshine, Kim, you know that? You also saw me when I thought one of those was him. You telling me it was just another code blue on that reef?"

Shane held his breath.

"Of course not. And if there had been another doctor there I'd have stepped aside. But there wasn't. I did the job."

Shane's heart had given a good hard jump at *Of course not* but the *I did the job* sent it dropping into his gut. Shane had already figured that what he and Jay had going wasn't just another fuck, and Shane had been there before, but the rest of it, that was all Joey and his treating them like they were halfway to married.

Joey was up on his tiptoes, pressing up against the sink. His foot slipped and slammed into Shane's ankle, making him grunt. Trying to catch himself, Joey knocked one of the mugs into the sink with a clatter.

"Shit," Joey whispered and ran for the door.

Aaron stood up and spun around to look at the window, and Shane was pretty sure the guy knew his boyfriend well enough to have filled in all the blanks.

"Joey, for Christsake, what the fuck are you trying to do now? You said after—"

Joey landed on Aaron's mouth mid-sentence. Shane knew the kiss was meant to shut Aaron up before he dropped a dime on Joey for eavesdropping, and that's all it was for a second. Then Aaron's hands lifted Joey under his ass and the kiss changed to something Shane felt like a punch to his gut.

It stole his breath, ramped up his pulse and hummed in his balls. It wasn't just the free porn of it, two hot guys kissing and petting right in front of him, it was how Shane knew that in that minute the roof could come down around them and neither Joey or Aaron would care. That kiss wasn't about anything but them. Fuck yeah, he was jealous, because he couldn't remember a kiss like that happening to him. Couldn't remember a kiss that wasn't simply a step on the way to something else.

Shane looked over at Kim. His face was still, but he was watching, not even pretending to look somewhere else as his friends reamed each other's mouths out. When he noticed Shane looking at him, Kim only raised those brows up into his hairline again.

Aaron had a hand in Joey's hair now, lips against his ear, muttering something that made Joey laugh. He smacked Joey's ass and Joey laughed again, feet dropping to the floor.

"Don't you have to work today, Chase?"

"Same shit different day. On at three," Aaron said. "Will I be bringing any in to you?"

"Not unless you're working a double. I'm not on until third shift. Double."

"I thought Rewatiraman liked you."

"He does. But his secretary makes the schedule and she's pissed because I was out a few extra days because of what happened. She takes it out on people who screw with her nice color-coded charts."

Like a brick to the back of the head, the realization hit Shane that he'd just dropped himself into the middle of Jay's life. He had a job and friends and coworkers and a fellowship to get and God knew what else. If anyone asked, Shane was blaming this crazy plan on the painkillers.

"What do you do for cash, Tex? Or do you have a pile of oil wells at home?" Aaron's attempt at a drawl made Shane want to punch him.

"Cattle ranch, actually."

Kim's eyes lit up with amusement, so Shane spun out the story.

"Daddy had a pretty big spread, but then he just added another 250,000 head, half of that from the H.W. Bushes. Biggest ranch in Bexar County." Shane imagined his engineer dad, in his business shirt and tie and mechanical pencils sticking out of his pocket, waving a hat as he drove a herd of cattle.

Aaron was buying it too. His brows drew together. "Kim told me you were the tour guide on the boat."

"Divemaster," Joey said.

"Oh, that was just a rebellion thing." Shane was pretty sure he could still pass for in his twenties. *Daddy threatened to cut me off* would probably be pushing it. "After what happened, I sure as shit ain't working for Sea Magic Dive Tours."

Joey was looking hard from Kim to Shane and then he smiled. "Nice."

"I thought it was pretty good stuff," Shane said.

Aaron realized he'd been played. "Asshole. So what are you doing?"

"He just got out of the hospital," Kim said.

"Ooo, defensive. How sweet."

"You'll have to excuse Aaron," Joey said. "He's been supporting a family since he could walk. He doesn't get the whole 'between jobs' thing."

Aaron looked like a lot of things, chief among them someone Shane would like to have on his side in a bar fight, but

151

he didn't look like the type to have a family to raise, but unlike Daddy's million head of cattle, Shane knew that what Joey said was true.

"So exactly what are you doing now?" Aaron said.

"Do I have to jump you again?" Joey asked.

"Is that supposed to be a threat?"

Kim cleared his throat. "Some of us didn't get to eat breakfast and don't particularly want to dry heave if you two put on another nauseating display."

At last Shane had something he could add. Maybe even something these two didn't know. "Don't want a repeat of the day we met."

"Right." Kim looked Shane's way, head tipped, brows down, and cracked a tiny smile. "And I left those anti-nausea wristbands on the boat. So give it a rest. Actually I think I still need some rest." His eyes got dark and intent.

Nope. Kim didn't look at Joey that way. Not at all.

"C'mon, princess." Aaron said and hauled his boyfriend out of his chair. "You'll have to play yenta later."

"But we forgot the coffee," Joey said.

"Take it with you," Kim suggested.

Chapter Thirteen

Kim wasn't sure it was possible, but things were even more awkward after Aaron and Joey left than it had been while they were there. When Shane slipped into the bathroom and shut the door, Kim suspected Shane was rethinking showing up out of the blue with no car and no plans. And Kim didn't want him to. He pushed off his scrubs and followed Shane in.

Kim had never bothered to replace the sliding glass doors on the shower with an easier-to-maintain plastic curtain. Now he was glad because there wasn't anything but steam to shield the view of Shane with his legs splayed and head tipped back under the spray. The water took a path Kim wouldn't mind following with his mouth, sliding down the long tendons in Shane's throat, catching on his nipples, gathering into a stream on his sternum to refract light from the red-gold hair under his navel, and then pool around his cock.

Shane took up a lot of space in Kim's shower, in his bed, and even in his brain. Right now, that was the way Kim wanted it. Shane filled the space that otherwise would have been full of worry over the looming decision about the rest of Kim's life.

Shane shook his head like a dog and opened his eyes. They went wide with surprise at first and then those lids came down, hiding whatever he didn't want Kim to see.

"Hey. I'll be out in a minute."

Kim shook his head and slid open the door. "Stay."

Shane made room for him, wincing as his shoulder came into contact with the cooler tiles along the back wall. Kim leaned in and lapped at the water under Shane's collarbone, drinking in the taste of the skin under the fresh water.

When Shane handed him the soap and started to step around to let Kim have the spray, Kim dragged him back so that they were pressed together, Kim's front to Shane's back. Not for the first time Kim wished he were five inches taller, but he could still comfortably reach Shane's shoulders, soap his pecs and play with his nipples. Shane sank back against him, and Kim spread his legs as far as he could to take the weight.

"Stay as long as you want." Kim licked Shane's shoulder.

Kim knew he wasn't Aaron with his need to find someone to take care of, and he wasn't stupid enough to get all doe-eyed like Joey about love, but Shane was a match for Kim in bed, and if having Shane around meant Kim wouldn't have to think about being stuck in Jacksonville for another two years, that was good. His vacation from common sense hadn't left him with a permanent scar this time, and Shane was a souvenir worth hanging on to for awhile.

Kim worked soapy hands down Shane's chest, rubbed hard on his thighs before making a teasing trail between them, thumbs grazing the heavy sac before gliding up the crack of Shane's ass. With a soft grunt, Shane reached back and gripped Kim's thighs. Scuba Cowboy's smartass remark about Kim needing a stepstool was far too accurate at the moment, because that was the only way Kim would manage to get inside him while standing in the shower. But Kim didn't want to stop touching Shane long enough to get a condom and lube, let alone find something to stand on.

At every stroke of Kim's hands, the muscles under Shane's

wet skin rippled with that vital current, warm and alive. Kim couldn't erase the memory of Shane cold and still on that reef, of the clammy, pale chest when he'd ripped open Shane's wet suit to get the paddles on bare skin, but he could have this one to go with it, Shane's heart pounding hard against Kim's palm, breath deep and strong as he fisted Shane's cock.

"Christ, Jay, I'm going to fall over."

There wasn't a lot of room, and Shane kept trying to spread his legs to get lower, closer.

"Grab the wall," Kim said.

Shane slapped a hand against the tile and held on to Kim's hip with the other one. Kim dropped his forehead between Shane's shoulder blades, concentrating on the sharp beat of Shane's heart, the thrust of his cock in Kim's fist.

"I want you to stay." The words were a whisper against Shane's back, and Kim wasn't sure they were audible over the rush of water and the echo of their quick breathing against the tiles.

"More. C'mon, Jay. Harder." Shane's hips jerked, trying to speed up Kim's strokes.

He tightened his grip, feeling the answer in the leap of electric current powering the muscle beneath his hand, the increase in the demand for oxygen driving the muscle to contract faster and faster. Kim used his legs to guide Shane's thighs together and pushed between them, finding soapy slick and hard skin to cradle Kim's dick.

Keeping a hand over Shane's heart, Kim felt the rush of blood and oxygen in his own body, endorphins and adrenaline. All the chemicals that made sex so good coupled with the prickle and pull on his balls, the hot friction on the needy skin of his cock.

Shane's fingers dug into Kim's hip. "Jesus."

Stay. Kim wanted to say it again, wanted to ask Shane with every thrust they made together. Ask him now when their bodies were flying on the high of all those hormones and neurotransmitters and everything made perfect sense. Was perfect, without Kim even trying, simply because this body answered his move for move. Shane's hand shifted from Kim's hip to his arm, fingers digging in deep enough to provide a little kick of pain that sent Kim rushing up to the edge. And he could let himself go over, because after last night, Shane had seen the worst of him and still met his gaze, still swallowed him in— there was nothing left to prove for either of them.

He bucked, dick angling up until he slammed against Shane's balls. Shane grunted again and his fingers wrapped even tighter on Kim's arm. The building tension snapped free, washing over Kim with an autoclave's heat, boiling from his dick as he pumped between Shane's thighs, bathed his balls with come.

"Fuck." Shane's voice was hoarse, hips shaking and then stilling as the spasms took over his muscles. Kim tipped his head to watch as Shane's final shot hit the back wall, and rubbed the last of the shudders from him, sliding gently on the come-slick skin as he softened.

Shane gave Kim's arm another squeeze before releasing him. Kim stopped stroking, fingers tingling with the memory of the satiny feel, his own cock still pulsing in satisfaction. When Shane reached for the handle on the door, Kim stopped him with a hand on his wrist. Shane turned to look at him, and Kim guided him down into a kiss with a hand on the back of his neck. Shane surrendered another groan, sending it deep into Kim's mouth, as hot big hands slid over Kim's back, down to cup his ass.

"Are you staying?" Kim asked.

"Okay. But you've got to get some groceries. I can't live on eggs and pizza."

Kim pulled his Jetta into the left-hand turn lane for Food Lion and waited for the arrow.

"Wait," Shane said, the urgency in his voice spiking Kim's adrenaline as he looked around for the crazed driver who was about to barrel into them.

As the traffic sailed by serenely, Kim rolled his eyes and said, "What?"

"We can't go shopping on empty stomachs. We'll end up with a lot of shit we don't want in the cart."

Kim had already figured that grocery shopping with Shane meant a lot of shit Kim didn't want ending up in his cabinets and had resigned himself to spending a lot more time at the gym.

Shane's stomach made a disgusting rumble.

"All right." Kim looked at his watch. Two thirty. "What are you in the mood for?" He glanced over at Shane.

"Korean." Shane licked his lips.

Kim ignored the leer. "Hope you like cabbage."

Shane wrinkled his nose. "Not unless it's deep fried in an egg roll. Hell, I don't like cabbage or potatoes and those are supposed to be Irish staples."

"So Korean and Irish are out." Which was good, since Kim didn't know of any Irish pubs in Jacksonville, though he was sure there had to be one next to the hospital.

"Well, the kind of Korean eating I want to do would be kind of rude at a restaurant." Shane winked.

The same wink that Kim had seen at the pool in Belize when Shane had baited him into scaring the other divers. God, Kim had been screwed then and he hadn't even known it, dazzled by blue eyes and a mountain of attitude. And now he had a hundred kilos of Texas in his bed, and was going to have biscuits for breakfast and food in the fridge and someone who would notice and maybe even care when he pulled forty-eight straight in the ER. And he'd fucking asked for it.

The blare of a horn shocked him into action, and he sent the car lurching through the intersection. Shane's hand slammed onto the dash.

"You okay?"

"Yeah. Just thinking. Umm, do you like Greek food?"

"That's fine."

Greek food. Shane staying. In Kim's house. He turned north on Phillips Highway and tried to call up a map in his head.

Shane staying. But for how long really? Shane would get bored. What had he said about college—nine years, six majors? How many different jobs? With that kind of attention span, Shane would probably be bored by Monday.

Monday. Decision day. Kim suddenly wished he had those wristbands on again. Because thinking about Monday without Shane as a distraction was worse than the engines on the boat. It was a long stretch of too much time to think about what had gone wrong, why Kim didn't have the right answer to make his life turn out the way it was supposed to. All these years of living in his head, it was suddenly the one place he really didn't want to be.

If Shane noticed that they made a complete circle of left turns before Kim pulled into the strip mall with Spiro's at the end of it, he didn't say anything. Kim hadn't been here in months, since takeout took forever, and he'd forgotten that he liked the dark wood, the cave-like nooks in the walls and the surly staff.

A nearly silent waiter took their order and vanished, leaving them alone in a cool dark silence with sweet teas in heavy plastic cups that utterly failed to look anything like glass.

There was a chess set on the table next to the bar, and without any regard for what the wait staff might be inspired to do to their food, Shane switched tables. He turned the board so that he faced it sideways and began a typical series of opening moves, following a basic Sicilian opening.

"I gather you play?" Kim asked.

"My dad does, Master level. Always kicks my ass, but he insisted that all of us learn—said it would teach us to think."

"Would this be the cattle-ranching dad?"

"The one who's an engineer on the side, yeah."

In his perfectly mapped-out life, Kim had been signed up for Chess Club in eighth grade, and two years later, he was able to hold his own in tournaments. Chess Club and tenth grade. That had been one of the first answers Kim had gotten that had fucked up everything about the world he thought he understood. That night in North Carolina with the club, saving money by sleeping with local families. And Kim learned that it didn't matter whether he'd signed up for Drama Club or Varsity football, he was always going to be queer, because what Tommy Ng did to him in that crowded house with half the team sleeping downstairs had been better and worse than anything Kim had dreamed or dreaded about in his life.

"Do you play?" Shane asked.

"I can."

"Pick a side then."

Shane had made white's light squares vulnerable as he'd played with the board, but Kim couldn't resist the challenge. He turned the white side to him and set about saving his queen. The worn-soft carved wood felt good and familiar in his hands, as did the patterns his mind found in the arrangement of pieces in front of him. He cleared the threat Shane had created, only to see the bigger trap just before picking up a knight to take Shane's bishop. Smart bastard.

Kim felt a stare hit his back and turned to see that an older man had come out to lean on the bar, watching them play. Shane turned with a wide smile and a genuine-sounding apology, but the old man just waved them on.

Now if Kim sacrificed his queen, Shane would be in check, his moves limited by the hedge of pieces around his king, but if Kim had missed an escape route, he'd be crippled for the rest of the game.

Risk or patience? He moved a pawn instead, provoking a cough from the man at the bar.

Their salads came and Shane took bites in between moves. Despite Shane's standard opening, his play now was erratic, and Kim felt like he was trying to anticipate the lurches of a drunk, as Shane sacrificed piece after piece instead of simply moving his king out of check. Two men were watching the game now, with an occasional comment in what Kim assumed was Greek.

Kim stared at the board, trying to see something he remembered from studying the game. His brain could provide picture after picture of games and the opposing move, but he couldn't see what Shane was planning. Always be three moves ahead, Kim reminded himself, but all he saw was the opportunity to take Shane's white bishop with no risk to himself. The waiter came in and after a brief discussion with the men at the bar, left their tray of food on the bar.

Shane glanced up and then back at the board. He moved his one remaining knight.

"Check."

Kim couldn't see the threat and then he did. But by saving Kim's own king, he had Shane mated.

Elation tingled in his fingers as he moved his queen. "Mate."

The man behind the bar made a distinct sound of disgust easily translated into any language. "Ah, you go too quick. Could have made even—a draw."

"I got hungry," Shane said, reaching for the tray.

"No patience." The man took the tray from him and distributed the food accurately. Egg and lemon soup and spanakopita for Shane, moussaka for Kim. "Always in a hurry."

"No focus," Kim said as the man took the chess set away, arranging it on one of the other tables.

"I've got plenty of focus." Shane leveled a stare, intent even with his eyes doing that half-lidded thing that kept Kim thinking about how Shane looked when he came.

"But you get bored."

"Yeah. I do."

Kim had known that. Had just told himself that in the car. This was one of Shane's many detours on his path to nowhere. Kim wanted him to stay, yeah, but everything had an expiration date. With Shane's attention span, that would be closer to the date on the eggs than on the ketchup.

Shane dipped the already fat-laden phyllo crust into the creamy tzatziki sauce, and stuffed it into his mouth. An action Kim found erotic for no discernable reason. He had reached out to wipe the white blob of sauce from Shane's chin before the realization that they were in a restaurant peopled by grim waiters and ancient Greek men who probably didn't approve of what "Greek/active" stood for in a MSM personal ad hit him like an ice bath. He gave it a halfhearted swipe and sat back in his chair, ignoring Shane's wide grin.

Kim took a forkful of his moussaka.

Shane nodded at the dish. "Mary's little lamb won't be following her around anymore, huh?"

Kim tried to remember what he'd seen Shane eat. He'd picked something off the pizza yesterday. "This a new-agey yoga thing? Are you a vegetarian?"

"Son, I'm from Texas. Not eatin' meat's a hangin' offense. But that's cows. Sheep and goats, no thanks."

Shane's slip into that drawl had become a shared joke instead of the way he'd used it like a shield on the boat. Kim thought of Aaron's face when he'd believed Kim was sheltering a cattle baron's runaway heir and almost sent some of the eggplant through his nose. He'd get a sinus infection if Shane didn't stop making him laugh when he ate.

When the bill came, Shane reached back for his wallet, but Kim slapped a fifty on the ticket. "I've got it."

"We'll split."

"Next time."

Shane studied him. "Is this a control-freak thing, a toppy thing or a Kim thing?"

"It's a you're-my-guest, don't-be-a-pain-in-the-ass thing."

Kim should have known Shane couldn't let it go that easily, and he was right again. As they got into a check-out line at Food Lion, Scuba Cowboy oiled his huge self around the cart and beat Kim to the cashier, handing over three fifties to cover the pile in the cart.

One thing Kim didn't need was a wife. He had money enough to handle the increase in expenses until Shane's ADD kicked in, but he understood Shane not wanting to be a kept boy. Even if the image of Shane in leash and a silver loincloth was entertaining—and a clear sign Kim needed a healthier outlet than online porn.

As they lifted the bags into the Jetta's trunk, Kim said, "You know, they're always hiring at the hospital."

"Sorry, Doc. Don't see me emptying bedpans, even for the chance of a little nookie in the storage closet."

"You watch too many medical shows." Kim hoped Joey never told Shane how much use Aaron got out of the ambulances. "I meant as transportation. They need people to wheel the patients in and out of surgery. It probably doesn't pay much but—"

Shane smiled at him. "Nah. I saved up a bit while I was working the tour. I might pick up a used car, look around a bit on my own. Never lived in Florida before."

"Jacksonville isn't exactly the top of the line in tourist attractions."

"I think you forgot what kind of ride I came here to find."

With a double shift, Jay would be back between three and four. Shane decided to pay him back for the hospitality with a good dinner, something that wouldn't go to shit if Jay was late. Jay liked pizza with meatballs, so a nice meaty lasagna would probably be a hit, and it was something Shane was good at.

After sleeping late and surfing through Kim's cable for a while, Shane went into the kitchen around noon. It took some scrambling to find stuff to cook in. The lasagna was going to have to be divided between a Pyrex bowl and a giant Pyrex measuring cup since Kim didn't have any kind of big rectangular pan like Shane would have used. He started by doctoring up the store-bought sauce and was sprinkling in some crushed red pepper when his phone started going off.

After the ticket to Jacksonville, a new phone was the first thing Shane had bought, but he could swear he'd only given the number to Jay—shit, and Braden. Which meant everyone in his family would have it by now.

He wondered which of them was calling to ream him out this time. Probably Megan. Pregnancy hormones were making her a real bitch. He didn't recognize the number, but he hadn't gotten around to programming anything in yet.

"Yeah."

"Hi. Shane." With a weird pause. Like the guy was trying out his name. The voice sounded kind of familiar.

"Who's—"

"It's Joey. We met yesterday."

"Right." But it explained nothing. Why the fuck would Joey be calling him, and how the hell had he gotten Shane's number?

"So I was thinking."

Fascinating. "Yeah?"

"One of my ex-boyfriends is an aquatics director at a state college in Tallahassee, and I called him this morning."

Shane was starting to grasp that Joey wasn't much of a get-to-the-point guy. He tucked the phone under his chin and stirred his sauce. It was giving off a nice nutty smell from the garlic he'd sautéed bubbling through it.

His lack of interest didn't matter, since Joey didn't seem to need any help with his side of the conversation. "So I told him about you and being a divemaster. Do you have certification to teach scuba? Or maybe lifeguarding? Or—"

"I can teach for PADI scuba certification, but lifeguarding, no. That would be a rescue diver. I mean, I have my CPR and all."

"Okay. Well, Noah gave me the name of this guy at UNF— um, the University of North Florida. You could probably teach a class there." Joey rattled off the guy at UNF's name and Shane made a sound like he was writing it down.

"Okay, thanks." The sauce began to spit big bubbles. Shane needed to start on the meat.

"And if you need anything, like a ride somewhere or—"

"Thanks, Joey."

Shane had a mound of grated mozzarella and ricotta and some noodles ready to be layered into his dishes when his phone rang again. He was already sick of his new ring tone.

"Hello?"

There was a hesitation and then another vaguely familiar voice. "Hey, Tex. Aaron Chase. You've got CPR and First Aid, right? You'd have to have that for the other job."

"Yes."

"You could probably pick up a few jobs teaching at the Y or doing a refresher for everyone at one of the clinics. Got paper?"

Jesus. Even Shane's family wasn't this bad. Or this obvious.

"Sure."

"Call over to the Red Cross and ask for Jeanie. Tell her I sent you and you're looking to pick up whatever jobs you can."

"I don't really—"

"Gotta go."

Shane remembered what Aaron had said to Joey about threats. What kind of pressure did Joey put on his boyfriend to get him to make that call? Or had Jay been the one to—no. Shane could not see Jay putting Aaron up to anything. Shane was certain Jay would rather cut off a ball than ask Aaron for help.

Rolling his eyes, Shane flipped his phone to vibrate. At least when his family got together to *Fix Things for Shane*, they had the excuse of well, being family. But two virtual strangers trying to step in because, what? They thought he was going to try to turn Kim into his sugar daddy?

After he had the two improvised lasagna dishes in the oven and had started on clean up, the phone started skittering on the counter. Shane dumped some soap into the sink and tried to ignore it. He didn't really need to know who else thought he was so pathetic he couldn't find a job—or even decide to look for one—on his own. His new phone had one hell of a powerful vibrate setting. The sucker was dancing on the counter. Shane made a mental note to carry it in his front pocket from now on.

He wiped his hands on the ass of his cut-off sweats and grabbed the phone just before it danced right off onto the floor.

"What?"

"Nice, bro. Once a brat…"

Braden.

"Did Megan have the baby? She okay?"

"No. But she's fine. And I'm fine too, thanks for asking."

"Sorry. It's just been—"

But it hadn't been anything. Getting up late, watching bad TV and making lasagna, even with limited resources, wasn't exactly the kind of high-pressure day that excused asshatted behavior.

"What?" Braden asked.

"Nothing."

"Nothing," Braden repeated. "How about where the fuck are you?"

After the doctor had looked Shane over in Texas and said he'd be just fine, Shane had told his parents he was going to take some time to rest up.

"Jacksonville. I told the units I was going to hang with a friend at the beach."

"Right. And did you give Mom a number?"

"I gave it to you."

"You could maybe check your email. Mom's sent you probably ten."

Jesus. He wasn't eighteen or even twenty-five. And he'd only gotten on the plane what, forty-eight hours ago?

"I'll call her."

"Do you need the number?"

"Fuck you."

"So your friend at the beach. That's your doctor, right?"

What the hell? Couldn't he fuck a guy a couple of times without the guy's friends and his family suddenly wondering who was going to be the best man? He wanted to spend some more time with Jay. Jay lived in Jacksonville. Shane lived...nowhere in particular. Which was why it made sense for him to be here. But trying to explain that just made it sound stupid.

"I'm staying with him, yeah."

"Mom didn't like him."

"Good. He's a little young for her."

"Ha. Ha. He seemed okay."

"Well, he's got the wrong equipment for you."

"Shane."

That same exasperated tone they all had. Braden didn't use it much which probably meant Mom was pissed, and Braden was hearing all about it.

"What?"

"Never mind. Just call Mom, okay? I gave her your new number, but she pulled that big guilt thing where she's going on about 'he'll call when he's ready' and 'I don't want to push'. I can't stand hearing it. So you'd better fucking call."

"Or you'll arrest me?"

"I'm sure someone in Florida law enforcement owes someone at the barracks a favor."

"No one told you to stay in San Antonio and buy a house down the street."

"No one told you to take off the second you were eighteen either."

"I'll call. Hey. How is Megan?"

"A total bitch. I hope she pops that kid soon. I feel sorry for Nick. I swear to God, I am never getting married."

"Me either."

"Good thing. You're already a bitch. You'll make some poor guy a lousy wife."

Shane looked at the kitchen, the sink full of dishes, the oven full of lasagna. Jesus Christ. "Fuck off."

"Call Mom."

Chapter Fourteen

When it got to be about six and no Jay, Shane cut himself a hunk of lasagna and stuck the rest in the fridge. It was pretty damned good, despite his having to improvise on the dishes. As the cheesy mass hit his stomach, lead weights settled onto his eyelids. He'd be worried about needing to roll back into bed after only eight hours of consciousness, but the doctor in Texas had said he'd probably be tired for a bit as his body finished putting itself back to rights.

He washed up his dishes and crawled into Jay's bed, time-zone shifts and lasagna and rhabdo—whatever the fuck all dropping down on him at once. He didn't shift an inch until he felt a warm breath on his ear and the sink in the bed as another body hit the mattress.

The warm breath turned into a lick and Shane stretched his neck out, because being woken up like this was way better than any kind of alarm clock he'd ever seen for sale in Brookstone.

The ends of Jay's hair dripped some, making Shane shiver as the drops hit the skin Jay had gotten all heated and sensitive with his tongue and breath.

"Is it raining in here?"

"Outside."

Something had been on Shane's mind when he fell asleep.

But Jay's mouth kept doing stuff to Shane's neck that was sending lots of blood flow south, and there wasn't a lot left to use for thinking. "I, uh, made you dinner."

"I saw it. What is it?"

"Lasagna."

Jay's chuckle huffed hot and cold over the wet spots on Shane's neck. "Lasagna?"

"You didn't have a—mmm—"

Jay sucked a tiny bit of skin in between his teeth, let it go and licked it again. "A mmm what?"

"Pan." Shane rolled onto his back because if Jay was feeling that oral, he could rock on down. A bit of stubble scraped over Shane's neck. "Still good though."

Jay moved his head and got at the skin just behind Shane's ear. "What?"

"The lasagna." Shane's mouth curved as he said it.

"Oh, it's the lasagna that's good. Want me to heat it up for you?" Jay's tongue dipped into the space under Shane's collarbone.

"You do that, Jay."

Jay licked lower, and Shane rubbed his hands down the cool wet skin of Jay's back. The muscles were tight as his uncle's wallet. Must have been a hell of a day at the office. Jay could use a little lightening up. "But you know, Jay. That's pretty cheesy."

Jay started to laugh against Shane's stomach, a tickle of vibration that turned into a snorting buzz.

Shane chuckled. "Did you just blow a raspberry on me?"

Jay lifted his head, his shocked expression showing in the light from the bathroom. He stared down at Shane's stomach as if they were reenacting a scene from *Alien*.

170

The laugh burst from Shane's gut with alien-spawn force. Reaching up, he rolled Jay onto his side and kissed the stillness off his face, laughed against his lips until Jay had to laugh too. Waves of it pouring over them warm and thick and almost as good as sex.

Shane wiped his eyes and flopped on his back. Jay hadn't rolled all the way into tears, but his full mouth was still curved up, smile bright and as unexpected as heat lightning.

"Damn, Jay. When you smile like that, you are still the prettiest thing I've ever seen."

Jay's voice held barely a trace of laughter, and Shane already missed it. "You're just saying that so I'll blow something besides a raspberry."

"Maybe. But it's true. You know, laughing makes sex better too."

"Is that so?"

"Yeah, same endorphins and shit, and it gets your blood moving."

"Mine's moving all right." Jay rolled on top of him. "I want to fuck you."

Jay hadn't asked him before. Just told him, and yeah, Shane knew that he liked Jay taking the reins like he had been, got harder than diamonds when Jay grabbed the back of Shane's neck and fucked into his throat. Asking felt different. It was the same quiet voice Jay had used when he'd said "Stay." It made Shane want to take Jay inside and wrap him up tight so he'd always smile like that, because that happy look on his face was too damned quick to disappear, like he was a kid whose toys kept getting snatched away.

Shane pulled Jay on top of him. "Yeah. I want that."

That smile got bigger, the sight twisting things deep inside

Shane, deeper than the sweet pull of arousal in his dick, ass and balls. Pleasure enough to curls his toes, the kind of so-fucking-good Shane couldn't ever get bored of. And that was scary as hell, because just like the best come of your life, that feeling couldn't go on. There was no hanging on to it, and it hurt like a bitch if you tried.

"What?" Jay's smile was gone, but Shane's gut kept pumping out that feeling, sugar rush and toothache all in one.

Shane shook his head. "Fuck me, Jay. Get that dick in me." *Fuck all this crazy shit out of my brain because I don't want to think about it anymore.*

"Just a sec." Jay swung off the bed and flipped on the light.

Where was he going? The lube and condoms were right next to the bed. When he came back there was a tube in his hand. He waved it. "Hydrocortisone, prescription strength." He uncapped it and broke the seal. "Call it a perk of getting fucked by a doctor."

"I can think of a few more." Such as Jay's damned accuracy in anatomy. Maybe Shane would have to do a random sample comparison. See if it was all doctors or just Jay's sense of dedication that made this so fucking good.

Shane moved his leg so Jay could get at the inside of the knee where it was the worst. The cream tickled a little, then cooled, soothing the itch that kept crawling under the welted skin. He found himself reaching to scratch it a million times a day, only to be brought up short by the memory of white-hot pain. With this cream on, Shane might be able to stand wearing a pair of pants for the first time in a week. "Thanks."

Jay capped the tube and pushed away from the bed again. "Got to wash my hands." He smiled again. The sexy, sweet curve on his lips popped there more easily this time.

Shane lay there with the blood pounding thick in his

throat. He wanted Jay smiling, and never wanted to be the cause of it stopping, but somehow Shane would be. Because he always was.

Somebody should stop this, say something about this being really good and all, but still temporary. But it wasn't going to be Shane. His conscience always took a back seat to the fact that he was a slut for pleasure and that wasn't going to change any more than the fact that everything he got involved in turned to shit.

Jay climbed on him, skin cool against Shane's sleep-warm body, but Jay's tongue teasing inside Shane's lips was hot. And after Jay had licked halfway down Shane's chest, he wasn't thinking about hot or cold or issuing fair warnings, but the fact that he was more than a little scared that if Jay's mouth sealed tight around Shane's cock he was just as likely to let slip a "Love you" rather than a "Suck me."

He didn't even notice when the slick bastard had grabbed the lube, but just as Jay's tongue circled the head of Shane's cock, a finger breached his ass, gliding too smoothly to be just covered with spit.

Jay's head bobbed in time with the thrust of his fingers. His hot throat closed around Shane's dick, and he held on to the edges of the mattress to keep from pushing deeper into that wet pressure.

Jay curled his fingers just as he pulled off to fuck the slit with his tongue, and for the first time in his life, Shane didn't want his dick sucked.

"Jay, stop. C'mon. Fuck me."

There was no arrogance in Jay's smile, no superior arch to his brow as he sat back on his heels and sheathed his cock. Shane was about to ask what had happened to the asshole he'd met on the boat when Jay pushed Shane's legs up and pressed that thick cockhead against his hole.

"M'ready." Past ready. Past wanting it, he fucking needed it.

Jay moved, just a bit of a stretch and then out, stroking all those nerves, until Shane felt every twitch of his muscles echo in his balls. It was different, not teasing this time, not a competition to see if Shane would roll over and beg for it, but almost like Jay didn't want to start because he didn't want it to be over.

Even when he pushed in, finally, *Christ, finally*, he kept control. A deep stroke, so deep they both moaned, and then he shifted, rolled his hips so Shane felt him everywhere, on every sensitized bit of skin, lighting up Shane's insides like Jay was made of pure electricity.

"Harder," was all Shane could say at first because he was going to come apart from it. From trying to hold that much sensation inside. Harder was the only way he could stand it.

Jay gave him that, grabbed Shane's hips and pushed his knees up to his ears. Shane thrust back, ass landing on Jay's thighs with every push up to meet his stroke.

And when Shane couldn't ask for it any harder, he started with "Jae Sun," the pronunciation as right as he could make it because fuck if his lips didn't want to blurt something else he'd regret when everything didn't feel this good.

This definitely wasn't a game anymore. Not the way they slammed together, hot and strong and desperate, like they were both trying to catch something that was slipping free, and if they let go it would shatter into a million pieces.

Jay bent down, gripped a handful of hair and fucked quick and hard, the new angle so perfect Shane had to squeeze his eyes shut to keep that feeling inside. It was pouring through all the cracks, spilling out in waves with the thrusts of Jay's cock inside him.

A sharper tug on Shane's hair. "Shane."

Jay had never said his name during sex. Just called him Cowboy. Shane jerked open his eyes to meet Jay's, and what Shane saw in them scared him all over again. Jay wasn't just fucking him with his dick, but with that look, that grip on Shane's hair, and then a kiss, hard and messy and wet with tongue. The twisting, dizzy roll in Shane's gut started again, an insidious curl of want, a helpless wish that he'd get this right, not fuck it up. Even with Jay's tongue wrapped around his, Shane could feel those words threatening to slide out. A promise, a plea.

When Jay stopped for breath, Shane whispered, "Harder, c'mon," in an act of self-preservation. Maybe if Jay went hard enough, deep enough, Shane could carry it inside him, hang on to this perfect fuck and be able to carry it around. Feel it over and over.

But that was nuts. Sex was fun and it felt good, but it didn't last, or everyone would be walking around with big smiles on their faces all the time and bars would go out of business.

Jay let go of Shane's hair and arched up, pinning Shane with a grip that held him steady as Jay's hips worked like a piston. Shane's cock was clearly on its own in this, and he brought his hand down to strip it fast. He was losing coordination, and he pinched his lips together and shut his eyes, cupping his hand over the head of his cock to give it a quick burn to match the fullness in his ass.

"Shane." Jay called him back again, forcing Shane to look at him, forcing him here and now, same as Jay had when Shane was dying on that tiny spit of sand and the only thing keeping him there was Jay's voice, dragging Shane back into his body.

And just like then it hit all at once, only instead of crashing into all that pain, this time it was pleasure, Jay keeping Shane locked in his body so he had to experience every last bit of it, every hot rush from his ass to his balls to his dick. The clench of muscles, the way his orgasm ripped free so hard it was tearing him loose at the root.

And when his cock had finished jerking, he dragged up his heavy eyelids because Jay was calling Shane again. Saying his name as a fierce, wild look stared back from Jay's dark eyes, no grimace, his mouth gone slack, cheekbones sharp as he made a few last thrusts. His eyes closed just as he swelled and jerked inside.

Shane lowered his legs, and Jay dropped his head onto Shane's chest, hand going to his hair, dick softening inside Shane's body.

Yeah, this was good. And he thought again about wishing he could hang on to it. If he didn't move, if time froze, then he'd never have to worry about how he was going to screw up the next perfect thing to come along.

Jay didn't pull out, just played with the damp strands of Shane's hair, lifting them off his sweaty face, off his neck. Every fresh rush of cool air made everything that much better. Yeah, yoga would be a lot more popular if this was the present moment they were always talking about.

"Someone should make a patch for this. You know, like nicotine. An orgasm patch. People could just walk around blissed out, high on sex. Peace on earth in a little patch."

Jay lifted his head but kept his fingers in Shane's hair. "You are a seriously weird person, Scuba Cowboy."

"Think about it. It's chemicals, right? So someone's got to be able to make them. Instant orgasm."

"You already have a patch. It's called your hand. Just go to the men's room and—"

"Nah. Not the same. It's better when someone's with you. Need another body to get the chemicals right."

"I must be high, because you almost make sense."

"Damn right."

The lasagna was good, even cold. Kim ate a chunk for breakfast, right out of the measuring cup. Shane hadn't been there when Kim had woken up, but there was coffee brewed and six feet of muscles stretching into interesting poses on Kim's lanai. The sight was a noticeable improvement over watching the morning news. He shouldn't be surprised that Shane had a Slinky for a spine, especially not after last night and all those chemicals. Kim had never believed in the bullshit claims about pheromones, about some tiny vestigial bulb in human noses, but something about the bendable redhead currently folded in half on the cement floor elevated sex from simple stimulus response to an all-out sensual onslaught. Watching him, listening to him, simply touching his hair and breathing in his skin intensified every sensation and release. Satisfaction still echoed deep, flooding all Kim's neural pathways with pleasure.

He put the lasagna back into the fridge and poured himself some coffee before going back to stand in the doorway. Shane looked up at him as he did something that made his spine form an arch like a hissing cat's.

"Hey. I'll put the furniture back when I'm done."

The plastic chairs were stacked in a corner. "Don't bother. They aren't very comfortable."

Shane moved into a perfectly held pushup, body a solid line of strength. "No kidding." A few more poses and he was standing, wiping his face with his yellow tank top.

177

Kim was sorry he'd interrupted. "I bought the set when I got back. When I remembered how much I missed sitting outside."

"I would have thought being stuck out there would give anybody agoraphobia."

"Nope. I remain issue-free, like I said."

"Issue-free with crappy furniture." Shane came into the kitchen and opened the fridge.

"Well, what would you suggest?"

Shane straightened up with a carton of eggs in his hand, the look on his face so stunned, Kim was afraid he was about to spend the morning digging a gooey mess of shell and albumen from the grout between his kitchen tiles. After a second Shane looked down at the carton in his hand and put it carefully on the counter. He didn't look up again.

"I don't know. I guess maybe a glider'd be nice."

"Glider?"

"Yeah. It's like a couch and a rocker, but it doesn't tip backward, it just swings a bit. It's relaxing. And comfortable." Shane was still looking at the eggs as if he expected them to hatch. "Um. I was gonna make an omelet. You want one?"

"I had some lasagna. It's good."

"Thanks," Shane told the eggs.

Kim replayed the previous night in his head. There was nothing he could think of that would have made Shane not want to look at him. Kim chalked it up to the frustrating inexplicable behavior of other people and took his coffee into the spare room to check his email.

There still wasn't anything from Portland and he couldn't shake the hope that somehow Dr. Warner would reconsider staying on at Sharp Memorial in San Diego. The final decisions could come as late as July fifteenth, two weeks away. He'd given his verbal commitment to remain at Shands here in Jacksonville yesterday, a few seconds before the call went for the victims of a three-car accident that were coming up from St. Augustine by helicopter. Spending the next ten hours trying to get some teenager's insides all back in the right places hadn't given him much time to reweigh the situation. The kid was down one kidney and a spleen, but he'd made it to ICU. Usually a surgery that long and complicated left Kim so wired he'd have to hit the treadmill for a few miles before he could go home to sleep. But knowing Shane was there, that what was waiting for him would be far better than exhausting himself on a treadmill, had washed the tension out of him as soon as he'd scrubbed out. Shane, a walking, talking, generous dose of Xanax.

Except for now, when he was hovering in the doorway, looking like his omelet had been garnished with salmonella.

"Hey." Kim looked up from the computer. He didn't have an email anyway—except for the usual offers to improve his wand of love. He'd have joked about it to Shane, but Scuba Cowboy had never looked less ready to laugh.

"Do you have to work today?" Shane asked.

"Nope. Tomorrow, third then first shift again."

"Okay." Shane remained half in and half out of the doorway, and with his height and broad shoulders, gave a pretty good impression of a door left ajar.

"What's the matter?"

Shane shrugged. "Nothing. Would you mind if I used your computer for a bit? When you're done, I mean."

Kim stood. "I'm done now."

Maybe Shane was an obsessed computer gamer—though how he'd managed to keep up that addiction while floating in the Gulf of Mexico Kim had no idea. Or maybe Shane was a compulsive gambler, desperate to check the scores of—whatever sport it was that people gambled on in late June. Baseball? For all Kim knew they were still playing hockey. At any rate, despite the hovering, Shane looked like he'd rather yank out his own tooth than get on the computer, but Kim stepped aside. He'd been planning—well, not a repeat of last night—but reciprocal blowjobs on the couch had seemed like a reasonable post-breakfast activity.

Shane's question stopped Kim at the door. "What do you usually do when you don't have to work?"

"Read medical journals online, go for a run outside unless it's hot, which it usually is since I'm almost always on nights. Sometimes I watch a movie." Kim went back to the desk and picked up his coffee mug. "Is this an interview? Should I have worn a tie?"

"No." The cinnamon freckles on Shane's cheeks disappeared under a flush. "I just didn't want to keep you from whatever it is you do. I'll be off in a second."

Whatever chore Shane needed to accomplish, it took about ten minutes, and hadn't improved his mood when he joined Kim in the living room. "It's all yours, thanks."

Perhaps there was a protocol for having a guest that you were also fucking that Kim didn't know about. Shane hadn't demonstrated an inability to express himself verbally before now, so if he wanted something, he'd have to ask. Med school and residency didn't leave much time for studying subtle social cues.

But after a few minutes of silence, Kim realized he much preferred the human Xanax version of Shane, laid-back, sarcastic and quick to laugh. If Shane still was fighting the aftereffects of the envenomation, Kim could send him back to bed. And wake him up again. Sleepy Shane had been a particularly satisfying dosage.

"What's wrong with you?"

"Nothing. What are you watching?" Shane stepped over the coffee table instead of around it like someone without particularly long legs would have to do.

"An unspeakably bad horror movie, starring a very young Jack Nicholson and a very old Vincent Price."

"Is that something you do a lot of?"

"Watch bad horror movies? Yes, it is. I like them."

Shane sat next to him on the couch, staring at the jumpy and badly lit black-and-white cinematography. After a minute, he eased back against the couch and some of whatever had been bothering him appeared to fade into the cushions.

"Does it get any better?"

"I don't know." Kim pointed at the red Netflix envelope on the coffee table. "I've never seen it before."

"You ordered it on purpose?"

"I like bad horror. And good horror. Sometimes—"

"It's a fine line," Shane finished. "Best one?"

"*An American Werewolf in London.*"

"Bad or good?"

"Mostly good, but also bad. Yours?"

"*Shaun of the Dead.*" Shane put his feet on the coffee table next to Kim's.

"You can't count that when it's satire." Kim prodded Shane's bare foot with his own.

"All right. *Night of the Comet.*"

"Still satire."

"You've seen it?" Shane's tone suggested he found the idea improbable.

"Valley girls battle zombies with Uzis?"

"They didn't have Uzis. Remember? 'Daddy would have—'"

"'—gotten us Uzis,'" Kim finished. "Right. But it's still satire."

"I think it's unintentional. But Robert Beltran was much hotter when he played Chakotay on *Star Trek: Voyager.*"

"Never saw it. I draw the line at sci-fi," Kim said.

"But then you exclude a lot of the best and worst horror. And it's science fiction, thank you very much." The diffident look was gone, Shane's eyes—which were either really that vivid a blue or the best long-wearing colored contacts Kim had ever seen—were bright and intent, hands moving as he argued his point.

The plot of the movie, such as it was, didn't require a great deal of attention to follow, and Kim found himself enjoying the debate. When was the last time he'd had to defend a position with something not medical? Exchanging insults with Aaron Chase was occasionally intellectually stimulating, but not the same as an actual discussion. "If the focus of the movie is on the traditional cathartic aspects of horror, then I'm for it, but when they turn it into barely disguised explorations of current social mores—"

"Did he just try to kiss him?"

"I can't tell." Kim tipped his head, as if a shift in perspective could improve on a film shot with an apparently nonexistent lighting budget.

The music had reached a clichéd crescendo when Shane said, "The other day, when you said stay, what did you mean?"

"I meant what I said. If you want to be here, stay." Kim thought about Aaron and the way Joey had just slipped in until Aaron didn't know what hit him. But like Kim had told the obnoxious prick, Kim didn't have the maternal instinct to nurture strays. Considered from a logical perspective, as long as Shane was a pleasant houseguest, there was no reason he couldn't stick around. There was a reason humans tended to clump together. It made things easier.

"How long?" Shane drummed his fingers on the back of the couch. It wasn't overt, but Kim spent enough time around nervous people to read the gesture.

"Until you want to leave." He considered what might dissipate Shane's apprehension. "If you're wondering, I would certainly tell you if I don't want you here."

"Like I said, I have some money saved. I'll pay my way."

Kim shrugged. "I'm not concerned with that."

"See, my family, mostly my mom—"

Kim had more than enough experience with the unwanted intrusion of family. "You don't have to explain anything. My family is overbearing too."

"Not like that. She—actually, she just wanted to know where to send my sister's birth announcement—when she has the baby, not my mom, my sister, I mean, and my birthday card."

After a moment of pronoun confusion, Kim deciphered the initial part of the statement, and then smiled. "Your birthday card?"

"It's next week."

"What are you going to be, twenty-five?"

"Thirty."

"Thirty?" Kim repeated. He was only a year older than Shane? It was true that medical school added ten years to your chronological age. Being a divemaster or a perpetual student evidently subtracted it.

Shane scratched the back of his neck. "Yeah."

"So your concern is basically about your address?"

"Mostly. But. I have to tell you something." Shane tucked his hair behind his ears. It seemed longer than it had just a week ago—probably because Kim was trying to see a thirty-year-old under the freckles and shaggy hair.

The color in Shane's cheeks suggested more embarrassment than a dire confession of some wrongdoing, but Kim picked up the remote and switched off the television. When Shane stood, Kim got the first flicker of alarm. Maybe it was something dire.

"I don't have the best track record for this." Shane spread his hands apart like he was telling about the one that got away.

"By this you mean...cohabitating?"

"Cohabitating?" Shane spat the word back like there was something obscene about it.

Kim was certain Shane's vocabulary wasn't limited to "shacking up", but he tried again. "Do you mean you're a bad roommate?"

"No." The word held a disproportionate amount of disgust.

Kim couldn't begin to understand what he wasn't understanding and he hated it. Confusion was as unfamiliar as it was loathsome, and he remembered why, despite the human propensity for pairing off, he had successfully avoided being befriended. For the most part. Unwilling to expose more of his efforts at communication to ridicule, he folded his arms and leaned back against the couch.

"What I mean is..." Shane's voice was back to normal, "...I'm a bad boyfriend."

Boyfriend. He hadn't thought of Shane that way, but that would be what to call him. Other than an assurance that Shane didn't announce himself as such if Kim's mother called, he didn't have any problem with the label.

Kim nodded. "Why?"

Shane looked up at the ceiling like he'd find the way to explain himself written up there in the stucco. As Kim followed his gaze he realized he was going to have to talk to the cleaning lady. It shouldn't be that dusty.

"I tend to get distracted. I don't stick around and when I try—it's—I don't want you to expect much. I'm not...reliable like that." Shane was still radiating disgust, but now Kim realized it was directed inward, and not at him.

Kim knew a lot of people considered a lack of fidelity a hardship in a relationship. But he wasn't one of them. Sex was exercise. It would be as irrational as being angry over Shane doing yoga with someone else. Of course, there was one important issue. "Provided we aren't acting based on an assumption of seroconcordance—"

"What the hell." Shane's tone landed somewhere between confusion and disgust.

Kim dealt with the easier of the two. "I mean provided we are taking proper precautions—"

"I know what the fuck seroconcordance means, Jay. I get tested. I'm negative and I don't—I never..."

But as Shane's voice trailed away, Kim knew they were both thinking of the deck chair, the thin skin of their cockheads, the slits, drenched in each other's come.

"I'm careful," Shane finished.

"Then I fail to see what the problem would be. My invitation doesn't have anything to do with an exclusive sexual arrangement." The angrier Shane got, the more Kim tried to put things calmly and clearly. He wanted this. Wanted to get out of surgery and know that Shane was here. Sexual compatibility aside, he enjoyed Shane's company, but since they weren't forming some kind of family unit, he couldn't see the problem. Shane said he preferred a variety of sex partners, and Kim didn't have time for it.

"Why are you pissed off? You're the one who brought it up."

"I don't know. Maybe I thought if we were going to have a relationship you'd care about more than seroconcordance."

"Well, I'm asking that you don't bring anyone here. My hours are unpredictable and—"

"Well it's good to know you might actually give a shit if you came in and found me fucking someone else in your bed."

Actually, Kim didn't know how he would react to that. He'd been thinking more about needing to sleep when he was off work, but he was smart enough to keep that information to himself. He looked down at his folded arms, a pose considered unacceptable by the granola-heads who did the hospital in-services on "client interaction", or as Kim liked to think of it "lectures on not treating the patients like a pile of potential organ transplants."

He unfolded his arms and let them rest by his sides. Shane had moved around the living room as the discussion progressed, but he stopped moving when Kim spoke.

"Can you explain to me exactly what the fuck you're so angry about?"

"I thought since you said you wanted me here, you might actually care whether or not I *was* here."

"I do want you here. But I don't want you to feel like you have to adopt some sort of role. I don't want a wife—or a husband for that matter. I want to have sex with you and I want to spend time with you."

"Like that? Just whatever?"

"Why not? Why should wanting you..." he tried not to smile when he said it, but it felt funny on his lips, "...to be my boyfriend mean you owe me fidelity?"

Shane looked like he'd rushed through two wings to get to a code blue only to find out someone had just pressed the wrong button. He walked over and sat on the couch, but not close enough to touch.

"If you really only meant to be here for the weekend, I apologize."

"Yeah." The word came out on a long sigh. "I do it all the time. Blow five hundred on an airline ticket for a booty call. Asshole."

There was still a disturbing sensation like discovering you were the only one in class who hadn't known about the reading. Kim wanted it gone. "So is the conversation over? Are you staying?"

Shane let out another sigh. "I want to. I just don't want to fuck things up. You don't think we should set ground rules or anything?"

"I was under the impression that you're more interested in breaking rules than setting them."

Shane turned his lips in and Kim waited for another explosion. He got a smile instead. "That's where the fun is."

"Where?"

Shane leaned in and put his hand on Kim's dick. "Between the rules."

Chapter Fifteen

Kim could have done without that frustrating conversation, but the compensatory blowjob was worth the previous discomfort. Shane held Kim off, alternating intense suction and gentle flicks, fingers shifting from the light tease of Kim's balls to the hard scrape of nails on his inner thighs. Just when sensation had him close to the edge, Shane stopped and started something different until Kim was desperate enough to try to remove his own spine so he could suck himself off. If this was the end result of a disagreement, he could see the appeal of make-up sex.

Kim wasn't entirely sure Shane had made up his mind to stay, but when he pulled the Jetta into the driveway a week later and had to squeeze around a truck that hadn't been there when he'd gone to work, the depth of his relief surprised him. He got out and looked at the truck. He wasn't particularly attentive to cars, but he'd be willing to guess the vehicle had been new about the time Kim started high school. They hadn't made cars in that shade of green for at least fifteen years.

Shane came out through the lanai door. "It followed me home. Can I keep it?"

"Provided you clean up after it and feed it. What's it get, six miles to the gallon?"

"Something like that."

"What is it?"

"My birthday present to me. And, the nice thing about a truck is that there was room in it for this."

Kim followed him in through the screen door. The plastic chairs were again stacked in the corner, and against the wall of the house was a vinyl-covered, metal-framed, couch-like object.

"Have a seat." Shane dropped down.

Kim followed more carefully. It did glide rather than rock, a relaxing movement that stirred a breeze while the cicadas buzzed in the yard. Not quite a deck chair out in the Gulf, but it was nice.

"Feeling seasick? I could run out and get you some more bands."

"Since you have that giant vehicle to fit them in. Sorry, I'm fine. You'll have to find another excuse to drive around in your present."

"So what did you get me?" Shane grinned.

"An invitation to blow me."

But Kim went into the house and got the box that had come in the mail yesterday. It would have been impossible to forget Shane's birthday. In addition to his daily variation of "I can't believe I'm going to be thirty", four cards had appeared in the mailbox, and before Kim had gone to the gym, Shane's phone had gone off roughly fifty times.

Kim hadn't wrapped the gift, and as Shane tore into the packing box the thought hit that Kim probably should have checked to make sure they sent the right one.

"*Night of the Comet*. I haven't seen this since I was twelve."

The disc was in the DVD player before Kim could get back to the subject of blowjobs.

The post-apocalyptic world was safe for shopping and big

189

eighties hair again when Shane leaned close to whisper, "I got myself something else for my birthday."

Since Shane's words were interspersed with the pressure of his mouth on the skin behind Kim's ear, he thought he should be forgiven for the assumption that it was a vibrating cock ring. Mind already on the possibilities and busy cursing his own lack of imagination in gift selection, it took some time before his brain processed Shane's next two words.

"A job."

Kim turned to face him.

"I heard about this Marine Research Institute at Jacksonville University and I wanted to check it out. It turns out the Oceanography Chair went to school with one of my advisors and actually was part of a project I worked on about three years ago, so now I'm teaching two sections of Rocks for Jocks: the Summer School Edition. Though I guess it's Wet Rocks for Jocks since it's actually Marine Geology. But if it goes okay, they might have a position for me in the fall at the institute."

"Wait. You're teaching at JU?"

"Well I will be as of Tuesday. The professor had to go on early maternity leave, a detached placenta or something, so yeah. I lucked out."

Kim was still trying to wrap his brain around the idea that when Shane had said he'd done nine years of college it hadn't been because he was failing but because he was getting an advanced degree. Or did they let people teach courses without degrees?

"You've got that surprised-to-find-out-I-can-spell-my-own-name look on your face again, Jay. It's not looking pretty for someone who wants to get his dick sucked."

"You said you went to college. You never said you finished

it."

"I finished a couple of things."

"I have noticed an impressive level of focus when I can capture your interest." Kim reached over and rubbed Shane's dick through his shorts, palm cradling the familiar shape, listening to the quick intake of breath whistle past his ear.

"Impressive, huh?"

Kim found the soft skin behind Shane's ear and licked down to his collarbone. He swore just the taste was enough to get him hard. He was going to have to apologize for laughing at that article on the vomeronasal organ in adult humans because this had to be pheromones. Nothing else could explain that one taste, one breath of his skin made Kim want to bury himself in this man, wrap himself in Shane until it was all he ever touched or tasted.

Kim made quick work of Shane's fly, mouth already watering in a Pavlovian response to the sound of Shane's groan. A drop of precome kissed Kim's palm as the blood beat under the soft, thin skin. "I'm definitely impressed."

Frustrated by the fact that people couldn't apply simple math to get in the correct line for an efficient checkout at Food Lion, Kim began filling out his check as they waited. "What's the date?"

Shane turned away from his meticulous study of the candy rack and tossed a king-sized Snickers into the cart. "July fourteenth. Bastille Day."

Kim wrote the date out and stopped again. Tomorrow was the fifteenth, taking with it the last tiny hope of sunny, non-humid San Diego, a continent away from disapproving parents.

The weeks had snuck by. Kim waited for that frantic feeling to hit again, the one that had sent him off to Belize, waited to feel the urgent pull of action, any action when confronted with only the second thing in his life he couldn't conquer just by knowing the right answer. He watched Shane contemplating the candy with the delight of the world's tallest four-year-old and felt his lips twitch. Fuck it. He hadn't thought about San Diego and the neighborhood he'd picked out and the layout of the hospital he'd fixed in his head for the past few days, and the reason why was bending over to pluck out the Snickers and substitute a Baby Ruth. Suddenly, it didn't matter if he couldn't put everything back together exactly the way he wanted. He was fine with here and now. The ridge under his tattoo didn't even throb.

"I'm getting half." Shane handed Kim two of his apparently endless supply of fifties. He couldn't possibly have gotten a paycheck from the university yet. Kim was starting to wonder if Shane was printing them off somewhere.

"Hey. Dr. McCormack."

Kim's head had gone up at *doctor*, then slowly processed the remainder as Shane's surname.

"Hey, Wayne." Shane nodded at a very tall teenager in the next checkout line.

The teenager waved and stuffed his earbuds back in, nodding in time to the music he'd chosen to permanently damage the auditory nerves in his cochlea.

As they put the groceries in the trunk, Kim said, "There are laws against impersonating a doctor."

Shane just smiled.

"What's it in?"

"Marine archaeology."

"Why didn't you tell me?"

"Because you medical types think you're the only real doctors." Shane slammed the trunk shut. "And quite frankly, hearing Dr. McCormack kind of freaks me out. It makes me think of white hair and scary beards. But there is something I wanted to tell you." Shane folded himself into the passenger seat.

Kim had figured out what emotions caused the unplanned shifts in Shane's accent. The slightly longer vowel sounds meant he was excited about something, so it probably wouldn't be a follow-up to his awkward declaration of his inadequacies as a boyfriend. Kim hadn't discovered any. Shane cooked, cleaned up after himself and still made Kim hard by just giving him a half-lidded stare. If that meant something was lacking in their relationship, Kim was all for it.

Kim drove out of the parking lot and headed for home.

Shane shifted in his seat. "I told you about the new Marine Research Institute, right? Well, they don't have an archaeology department and they've been getting a lot of requests for one. There's a sudden interest in Pre-Columbian culture. Probably because of—"

"And?" Kim prompted. Sometimes he enjoyed Shane's discursive rants about academia—and with closer consideration Kim should have realized he had an advanced degree—but he wanted to get to the end of the story before they got out of the car. He was working third shift and he'd really hoped they could fuck before he went in.

"And there aren't a lot of people with the double doctorate in—"

"Wait. You have two Ph.D.'s?"

"Yeah." Shane passed it off as if it were as common as having two nipples. "So the Oceanography Chair—remember I told you we met on a dig? He came in to see me today and asked if I'd be interested in setting up a curriculum as part of the new institute."

"And you would."

"Hell, yeah. I haven't had a chance to work in the field in almost two years. I'd still have a class load, but there'd be fieldwork. The institute is all about career focus. But..."

Kim had known there would have to be a catch. Otherwise his Scuba Cowboy/Indiana Jones would have jumped at the offer.

"They want a three-year commitment to the project," Shane finished.

For Shane, three years probably sounded like a lifetime.

Kim pulled into the driveway, but neither of them got out of the car.

Shane turned to face him. "What do you think?"

The question held a surprising paralysis. As much as Kim wished he could pin it on the lack of familiarity with people asking him for non-medical advice, he had no idea how to answer.

"Why?"

"Jesus, Jay." Shane thumped a hand on the dashboard.

Definitely the wrong answer. But wanting Shane to accept a commitment just because Kim had decided he liked having a boyfriend wasn't the right answer either. "I mean, it's your career. Why should my opinion matter?"

"Seriously?" Shane got out of the car.

Kim squeezed the steering wheel. Why wasn't there a manual or a course or a diagram for this? He got out.

"Why do you get angry when I'm trying to figure out what you mean? Why don't you just tell me what you want?"

194

"Pop the trunk, Kim, my ice cream is melting."

Kim leaned against the trunk. "Three years is a long time."

"And it's not getting any shorter while we stand here." Shane looked like he was considering wrestling the keys away but shoved his hands in his pockets instead.

"And you want to know if I think you have the ability to last at a job for three years, or are you asking if our relationship will continue that long?"

Shane threw his hands up in the air. "Yes."

"How could I possibly know?"

"Forget it." Shane reached for the keys.

Kim held on. "No. I realize I don't have two Ph.D.'s but try to use little words and explain exactly what the fuck the problem is."

"Are you angry?"

"Yes."

"Well, hot damn." That drawl, thick and cloying and infuriating.

"Getting angrier."

"Go ahead. Maybe then I can figure out what the fuck you want."

"I told you. I want you here. And that has nothing to do with your job. Or even whether you have one."

"So then fucking act like it."

"What does that mean?"

Shane put his hands on the trunk on either side of Kim's hips and leaned in. "It means I want you to care about my job. I want to know if you care whether we'll still be fucking our brains out in three years."

Kim reached up and pulled Shane's head down. Kim knew

195

this body well by now, knew the instant Shane decided he was going to let his head be dragged down, felt the yield in his muscles, in his breath. Kim meant it to be a rough kiss, a way to let Shane know that no matter how angry he made Kim, the want was still there. But Shane opened his mouth, lips warm and yielding, and Kim could only lick inside softly. Shane's hands landed on his hips and held on as Kim's thumbs slid down Shane's jaw, dragged down to the hollow of his neck. Shane groaned, but Kim heard as much frustration as it was arousal.

Shane pulled free. "I wish that answered everything."

"I wish it did too." Kim turned and unlocked the trunk, lifting out bags of food. For a second he wasn't sure Shane would follow him in, convinced himself that the next thing he heard wouldn't be Shane's truck starting up as he disappeared. Kim unlocked the door and headed for the kitchen, swallowing his own frustration until his ears rang so loudly he wasn't sure if he was hearing the scrape of Shane's feet behind him.

But he was there. He dropped the bags he'd carried on the counter and the floor and tucked his hair behind his ear, as if he couldn't be properly irritating with his hair hanging in his face.

"So now what?"

"I'm thinking."

"Christ, Kim, either you give a shit about me or you don't." Shane turned to reach into a bag. "You know, fuck it." He headed for the door to the lanai.

"No, fuck you. Don't I get a minute to answer?"

"Sure. I can even hum the theme from *Jeopardy*. Take your time. I'm sure I fit somewhere in your oh-so-full brain." The door shut behind him with a bang.

Kim listened. The screen door didn't open and he let out a

deep breath.

He put away the stuff that had to be refrigerated. He'd never tried to have a discussion like this before, had no idea what to say. He could understand what Shane wanted, but there was no way he could respond the way Shane expected.

Declaring "I want you, I'd miss having you here if you decided to leave, but..." he looked down at the Queensrÿche emblem on his wrist and finished the thought, "...I don't believe in love" was a pastiche of bad song lyrics and not a statement that would end with either of them wanting to have sex before Kim went to work.

And if that was all he'd wanted, Kim could have faked a response that would get Shane there. But it wasn't just about sex. Kim wouldn't have offered Shane a place to stay if their interaction was limited to satisfying each other's libido.

He still didn't know exactly what he was going to say, but he stepped through the kitchen door. It was after eight, and a typical evening-storm sky sucked the colors out of the sunset. Humid air clogged his throat.

Shane sat on the glider, sliding it back and forth, but without the kind of force his exit had led Kim to expect. His hands were cupped behind his head, legs stretched out, using just his heels to propel the glider. He didn't turn, and Kim studied his profile. There wasn't a logical explanation for why Shane McCormack and his two Ph.D.'s had come to matter so much in Kim's life. He was physically impressive and charismatic, with those freckles and the wide mouth and the wink in his eyes, but Kim knew it wasn't just Shane's appearance that had Kim out here trying to put words to something he didn't understand so he could keep looking at that face. And part of what made finding those words so hard was that if he didn't—as Shane had eloquently stated—give a shit, Kim wouldn't have hesitated to say whatever would get him what he wanted: a return to the easy way things had been before the Oceanography Chair at JU had decided he needed a marine archaeology department in his new institute.

Kim sat on the glider and let Shane rock them as they both stared out into the murky gloom. "I think it's a great offer. And I think they must really want you to ask for that kind of a commitment."

Shane snorted and the glider stopped moving. "Thanks."

"But I don't want you to base your decision on me."

"Did I say I was going to?"

"You asked what I thought."

"I sure did," Shane said, inflecting the words like they were the punch line of a joke. "I want the job."

"Okay." Kim might not be as good at conversational cues as he was at finding an elusive vascular trauma, but he still knew they weren't done.

The sky spit a little rain with a halfhearted attempt at thunder.

Shane started rocking again. "Did you always want to be a doctor?"

"It's what I want now."

"But did you always want it? I mean when you were a kid, is that what you wanted to be?"

Kim didn't remember any other future plans. Even if his parents had chosen it for him, he had wanted it, and he was good at it, and he liked it. "Yes."

"I've never had that. I've never known what I wanted past getting it."

The glider stopped. The rain started again, fully committed now, flattening the grass to silver in the light from the driveway.

"This. Us." Shane turned to look at him. "It's the closest thing I've ever had to figuring out what I want. And I want that job."

"So you should take it."

"But I don't want to live here in Jacksonville if I'm not with you."

This was easier than Kim had thought it would be. That's what he wanted too. Maybe it wasn't so complicated.

"You are."

"So what I'm saying, what I'm asking, is if this ain't gonna work, I need to know it now."

Kim wished he could lie. "But how can either of us possibly know that now?"

"I think you can. I know I do. Why the hell else would I let my peanut butter fudge ice cream melt on the kitchen floor?"

"I put it away."

"See? That's why...why I love you, Jay."

Kim's brain now flooded with a million ways to refute Shane's statement. They'd known each other less than a month. They'd been through an intense ordeal together. And the concept of love was nothing more than a social construct. But Kim didn't say a word. He couldn't look at Shane, stare into those blue eyes and tell him he didn't feel what he said he did.

"So, you in?"

Kim couldn't think of a single reason why not. "I'm in."

Chapter Sixteen

He had to leave for the hospital in less than an hour, but Kim still wanted to take his time. Shane was less than cooperative. There was a distracting amount of licking his chest and squeezing around Kim's dick. He pulled out to give himself a second to catch his breath.

"Somethin' wrong, Jay?" Shane winked.

"Smug bastard, aren't you? Roll over."

Pinning Shane on his stomach with hands at his shoulders, Kim treated his tongue to a game of connect the dots with the constellations of freckles on Shane's back.

Shane squirmed under him. "Fucking tickles."

"Good." Kim shifted his grip to shoulder and hip. He could map the galaxy in less time than it would take to cover all those spots, from tiny bits of gold to darker warm brown. He'd have to make sure Shane went to the dermatologist regularly. Melanoma could be deadly unless it was caught early and all that sun exposure made him a prime candidate. Kim's lungs felt compressed, and he couldn't fill them with air. The thought of Shane with cancer, with any of the million deadly pathologies that plagued humanity, compressed Kim's lungs as surely as a hyperbaric chamber—without the benefit of equally compressed air. Dizzy from the sudden reduction in oxygen, he tightened his grip on Shane's body.

Shane turned his head on the pillow. "You all right?"

The long drawn out *i* loosened the grip panic had on Kim's diaphragm and he smiled.

"I'm fine." He drew his tongue along an almost-perfect hexagon. "You really ought to wear a hat."

Shane's body shook with a laugh. "In bed? Whoa. Ain't you a kinky son of a bitch?"

In bed would be just fine, but— "I meant when you're outside. When you're doing all that fieldwork."

"Oh. I always seem to lose them."

The brief bout of anxiety had taken a toll on Kim's hard-on, but he leaned up and breathed in the smell of Shane's hair, licked the sweat off his neck, and the pheromones flipped all the right switches.

He scooped up Shane's hips and drove back into the tight heat with one long stroke. Pressed tight against him, Kim slid an arm down over Shane's shoulder.

"I'll glue the fucking hat on." Kim arched back and drove in hard enough to pull a grunt out of Shane.

"Okay." Shane held tight to his arm. "Glue's good."

Kim fucked into him, thoughts finally fading into the rhythm of moans and tingling friction. Shane reached back an arm and grabbed at Kim's thigh, pulling him tighter and tighter.

The edge was right there again, release so close it lay metallic and sweet on Kim's tongue, and he realized his mouth was sucking hard enough to avulse a piece of Shane's shoulder.

He raised his head. "Sorry."

"Stop being sorry. Just stop stopping."

But since Kim already had, he took advantage of the opportunity to turn Shane onto his side, moving that wide, smiling mouth into kissing range. Kim's hand closed around the

201

raised lines on Shane's knee and thigh, and he let go immediately. Shit.

Before he could apologize again, Shane murmured, "'S okay. It's a lot better."

Kim hiked Shane's leg up, thumb dragging across one of the welts as Kim drove the breath from them both with a hard thrust. He wanted to trace those lines with his tongue the way he had Shane's freckles, kiss the scars that night had left on Shane's body. Remember they hadn't killed him. He was still here.

Kim moved faster now, because this didn't have to last. He got to do it all over again for an endless bunch of tomorrows. He moved Shane's leg toward his head, and the groan from Shane's mouth shook the whole bed.

"Damn, Jay. Just like that."

Kim dropped an openmouthed kiss on Shane's lips. "You got it. Baby."

And when Shane grinned back at him, Kim did something he couldn't ever remember doing before in his life. He winked.

He had seriously underestimated the power of a wink. Shane groaned again and fisted his cock, panting. "Fuck, gonna come."

The low deep whine in Shane's throat rolled down Kim's spine and went off like a grenade. His hips stuttered and his eyes squeezed tight as he tried to hold on to make sure Shane came with him.

Shane sputtered a refrain of *fuckfuckfuck*, the rough pleasure in his voice making it even harder for Kim to keep moving steadily, to hold back the flood in his balls.

"C'mon, baby." The word slipped out like it had on the reef. Nothing playful about it now, not life or death but it sure as hell felt like it to hang on that edge with every nerve urging his body toward release.

Shane's ass tightened, quick hard pulses around Kim's dick, and Kim let go, snapping his hips forward, tension spilling free in sweet bursts. Shane's muscles squeezed him again, pulling Kim in, keeping him deep inside, his body and mind linked in a way they usually only were when he did surgery, a clean crisp connection that let him see everything, solve everything. Shane was onto something with his instant-orgasm patch.

"Hey." Shane's voice was soft.

Kim blinked and looked down. Shane's smile was soft as his voice, almost hesitant.

"Hey." Kim turned and dropped a kiss on the healing welts. One of gratitude, because without them, Kim knew they wouldn't be here. Without the pain and the fight to keep Shane alive, Kim knew he wouldn't have this. And he might not need it, not in the way that he needed air and food and water, but God, he wanted it. Wanted all he could get of Shane's warm body and warmer smile. Wanted to sit on the couch and try not to think about how much butter Shane had dumped on the popcorn as they critiqued bad horror films. And thanks to the Oceanography Chair at JU, he'd just gotten the extended warranty on it all. Three years of protection against Shane's ADD, against the sight of Shane tucking his too-long hair behind his ears while he stammered through an explanation of why he was off to find his next distraction.

A warm tongue teased Kim's right wrist and he looked down again. Shane licked the long black spike of ink, and Kim shivered. Not with sensation, the scar was too thick for that, but with actual cold. As if the pressure on the skin reminded him of how cold it had felt.

Shane gave him an inquisitive look. "What's it feel like?"

"Pretty much nothing. Just skin. Why?"

"Well, I figured if you were kissing my scars, I could kiss yours."

A wave of cold roared over him. So cold. Thick and black and empty, and Kim didn't want this connection with his body anymore. He pulled his arm away and gently lowered Shane's leg.

"How much did it hurt?"

Kim forced himself to remember that Shane couldn't know what was underneath, that he was only talking about the tattoo.

"I don't really remember. Why? Are you planning to get one?"

"Me? I just freaked out about my dream job because it came with a three-year commitment. You think I could commit to a tattoo for life?"

"Guess not." Kim should be in the shower. The rain would slow traffic and he'd need to leave earlier. But after he'd flushed the condom, he went back, stretched out next to Shane and tried to soak up some warmth to chase away that icy memory.

Shane put his arms around him and rolled on top, tangling their legs and forcing heat on him with the sheer size and weight pressing him into the mattress. He rubbed a hand down Kim's side.

"Damn. Guess you should turn off the a/c. Rain really cooled things off."

Kim hid a choked laugh in Shane's shoulder.

"You all right, Jay? Want me to drive you so you can sleep on the way?"

"It's only twenty minutes."

"Okay. I'm going to go in early and talk to Dr. Jorgensen."

"So you're going to take the job?"

"Yeah."

"Good." He could have five more minutes of this, of heat and life pressed tight against him. "I won't see you tomorrow then. I've got to go back in at three."

"Damn, you really pissed off that secretary, didn't you?"

"She hates to use white-out. It messes up her pretty colored charts."

"Ask her if she hyphenates anal-retentive control freak or if she prefers it as one word."

Shane's warmth had soaked into Kim's bones.

He smiled. "I'll do that."

Kim had just gotten home and was going to squeeze in some sleep while Shane was off accepting his new position when the doorbell rang. If it was Aaron, he could go fuck himself. And if Aaron and Joey had gotten into another fight, Joey could find somewhere else to calm down. Kim was tired.

He yanked open the door to find a bored postman with a clipboard. "Kim, Jae Sun."

"Close enough."

The mailman handed him an envelope stamped with registered and certified. Kim signed off on the guy's clipboard and looked at the return address.

Sharp Memorial Hospital, San Diego, CA.

He had to sit down in the hall.

Chapter Seventeen

Shane had been through his share of summers in San Antonio, stretches where anything under a hundred was a cool down, but by the end of August, Florida was downright disgusting. He was swimming through steam as he checked out the dig site his class was working tomorrow. Maybe he could get them to start at dawn, and then remembered he could do whatever the hell he wanted now that he was in charge. Two months of having his own department and sometimes he still forgot he was the boss. It wasn't as fun as it sounded. He had a hell of a lot more respect for the people running things than he used to. He could stand to be back taking orders, without anything to worry about but stretching grid lines across the silt on the bottom.

They'd barely get their feet wet on this one though. Divers doing a safety check on bridge pilings had found an older foundation, but Shane was betting it wasn't anything earlier than Spanish occupation, and late seventeenth century at that.

He lifted his shirt where it was stuck to his back and decided everything that wasn't ready would keep till tomorrow. The skin under his bandage itched, and he wanted to get home and look at it. Then maybe he could decide if it was either all right or the stupidest thing he'd done in thirty years of fucking up. He'd sure as shit have told anybody else they were a moron for doing it.

Thinking about it now made him more than a little dizzy, or maybe that was the heat. He climbed into his truck and cranked the a/c, careful to keep from pressing his freshly tattooed shoulder into the seat back. It didn't hurt—not compared to getting up close and personal with a Portuguese man-o'-war. With that for a comparison, the hour he'd spent on the table at Missing Ink? this morning fell under the category of irritating. Didn't mean it didn't sting now with sweat soaking through. Or that he didn't get a reminder every time he pushed back against the seat.

Yeah. It had been a crazy idea, but somehow, he'd felt he had to do it. And he hadn't just walked in to the first place in the phonebook. He'd checked around online, even asked one of his well-inked students for a recommendation. And he'd gone to two different professors in the Asian Studies department to make sure he had the letters right.

As soon as he got into the house, he dumped the mail and stripped off his shirt and the gauze pad. He tried to get a good look in the mirror, but with it being on his shoulder blade, it didn't quite work out. He ended up snapping a picture with his phone.

The skin was swollen and red, but the letters looked right. The same ones he'd been studying since he got this crazy idea.

He sent the pic to Braden—it wasn't like Braden had never done anything stupid, and unless he had hidden talents in reading Korean he wouldn't know what it said anyway—and started sorting the mail.

There was the birth announcement from Megan, because the call at three a.m. back on the tenth wasn't announcement enough. Amanda Lynn Moore was a cute little thing, even if she did already have a head of red hair, poor kid. The picture went in his wallet. Jay's mail went on his desk.

It wasn't as if Shane was looking through Jay's stuff. Shane had gone online and found a cute set of little sea animal bath toys to send back home and he needed a pen. So he moved some papers around and there it was.

A one-way ticket to San Diego. First class. Not even an e-ticket. Paper. The kind you had to pay extra for.

For a minute, Shane was back on that reef, gasping for breath, insides feeling like someone was taking them out with an ice cream scoop. He shut his eyes and he could still see that damned ticket.

Since he couldn't unsee it, he unfolded the letter that had come with it when his search knocked them from the stack of envelopes.

The good folks at Sharp Memorial Hospital were so awfully sorry about the late notice on Dr. Kim's fellowship and the mix up over Dr. Warren's retirement that they were waiving the interview and sending him this first-class ticket, and they looked forward to him beginning at Sharp Memorial on September fourth.

Shane's hands and feet went cold and the fucking tattoo burned. Was the little shit just going to fucking disappear? *Yes, Shane, it's a great job. Sign that three-year contract while I head to the other side of the country where this time I don't have to worry about your dumb ass following me.* With a doctor's hours, Shane might not even notice that Jay was gone for days. Wow. Shane could really take home the epically stupid award this time.

It had taken all Shane's yoga-honed flexibility to get a fresh gauze pad on the tattoo. He ripped it off, grabbed a shirt from the top of his drawer. Unless he picked up someone who read Korean, maybe no one would ever find out Shane had been stupid enough to get a guy's name tattooed on his back.

He'd aimed the truck toward the hospital without even thinking and pulled off into a strip mall when he realized that not only would he probably be waiting around half the night until Jay got out of surgery, he didn't want to talk to the asshole.

He knew two things that a guy needed when he'd been fucked over this good. Liquor and dick. And he was pretty sure he knew someone in Jacksonville who could tell him where to find both.

Jay's buddy Aaron had known where to go all right. Down to what end of the bar to sit at depending on the time of day. So it wasn't his fault Shane ended up sitting on the fucking glider with Old Grand Dad and a shot glass instead of balls-deep in somebody who wasn't an arrogant trauma surgeon who didn't give a shit about anyone but himself. No, that was good old Dr. Kim's fault too. He'd found the bar, found the guys, found one with an ass that even put Joey's to shame and then he'd bought the guy a drink as an apology and headed for the liquor store across the street.

And it wasn't just that the guy wasn't snarky, sneaky and hung. Shane just didn't feel like taking the reins. Didn't know if he wanted to anymore. The side of him that had been quick as a whip to get a guy face down with his pants around his ankles didn't seem to want to come out and play.

The shot glass, though. That was Shane's idea. Because he was keeping count. He figured six or seven would fix the scooped-out feeling in his gut, and still leave him able to rip Jay a new one when he got home. What Shane hadn't accounted for in his plan was that after five, counting got to be a bit tricky.

Which is why he woke up all-over sore with a face full of sunshine as it flooded the lanai.

He squeezed his eyes shut again and took some inventory. The aching head—that was courtesy of Old Grand Dad. The stiff bones, that was courtesy of sleeping on a glider that was a good two feet shorter than he was. The sharp pain on his left shoulder was because he had apparently unknowingly donated the part of his brain that kept him from doing stupid things like getting a guy's name tattooed on his body. But the empty feeling in his gut, the one that felt so big he was afraid he could fall in it and get lost for a week, that was all courtesy of Jae Sun Kim.

He managed to drag his watch up to his face long enough to figure out that he had six hours to pull himself the fuck together before he had to be out in the sun with twelve teenagers on their first dig.

His head wasn't too bad if he kept his eyes open. And he'd only ever puked from drinking that one time when Braden took him out for his twenty-first birthday. Some water and aspirin and a shower and he'd be fully functional.

He sat up and realized there was a blanket on him, a hand-crocheted kind of thing like the one his grandmother had made for him when he went to college. His foot had gone through one of the looped spaces in it, and by the time he'd untangled himself he was aware of another obstacle between him and the salvation of water and aspirin. Kim leaned in the doorway, managing to drink coffee and still keep his arms folded and a superior look on his face.

"Sleep well?" Jay asked.

"Fuck. You." Shane wasn't having this conversation without his water and aspirin.

Jay was smart enough to get out of his way. The fucking

plane ticket was on the kitchen counter, but Shane shut his eyes and found the fridge anyway. Orange juice would work too, right? Were there electrolytes in orange juice? He'd ask Jay, but he probably wouldn't tell him, any more than he'd told Shane about moving cross country in a week.

Shane drank the juice from the carton.

"I assume that's what this is about." Kim had come up behind him. Shane looked at the ticket again. There was a pill bottle next to it.

"Aspirin?"

"Acetaminophen is easier on your stomach. Especially if you're going to drink that much orange juice."

Shane knocked four little pills from the bottle and sent them down with some more of Florida's much-celebrated orange juice. It stuck in his throat like he'd swallowed a toad. Christ. It wasn't bad enough that he'd have that tattoo forever, at least he couldn't see it. But if he was going to get all bent out of shape over orange juice because it would always remind him of Florida and Jay and this little house and the glider and the lanai—that just fucking tore it.

He slammed the juice down on the counter and walked away.

"Where are you going?"

"Not to San Diego. Have a nice trip. Don't worry. I wouldn't have followed you even if I hadn't taken the job."

"I'm not going either."

Shane stopped. Good thing too. The house wasn't that big and he wasn't ready to face the sun. He turned to stare down Kim in the space between the kitchen and the living room that might be called a hall if you were used to living in a shoebox.

"Huh?"

"You heard me. If you had bothered to look at the letter while you were digging through my stuff—"

"I was not digging through your stuff. I needed a pen."

"—you would have seen that the letter was dated July fifteenth."

"Wow. And here you still let me keep your sheets warm all the way through August. Thanks."

Kim didn't stop. "And that I had to give them an answer right away. I did. I said no. Six weeks ago."

Shane was surprised at how much better he didn't feel. Because he didn't want Kim turning down what he'd worked for his whole life, and if Kim had bothered to ask, Shane would have fucking told him that.

"I'd never have wanted you to do that. But hey, I didn't know shit about it. Why? Because you don't tell me anything that goes on in your head. You fuck me, we live together and we eat together, and I never know anything you're feeling unless it's horny."

Kim looked down for a second then met Shane's eyes again. Gaze steady, tone even. "Do I get a turn now?"

"No, you don't get a turn. You get pissed and take one. You do something, say something that shows you feel something. And I mean more than just liking the way my ass feels on your dick. Do you even have feelings, Jay?"

"If I didn't, I'd already be in San Diego," he snapped. Score one for Jay.

"Then why didn't you say something to me?"

"Fine. You want to know what I'm feeling? Frustrated. Pissed off. I am sick of feeling like I have to prove something to you because you need some kind of external validation of your worth."

"I'm the one who needs that? For Christsake, Jay, you lie to your parents. Hell, the whole reason for you even picking that job was because you wanted to get away from them so they'd never find out you're gay. Don't give me that outside-approval shit."

"You don't understand what it's like in Korean culture."

"And why not? Because you don't talk to me about it. And yeah, I might not know shit about what it was like to grow up in your world, but I know what it was like to be a skinny gay redhead in Texas. I can run pretty fucking fast."

Shane could sense the front door right there. Smell the air and the space leaking through. His keys hung up right next to it. There wasn't anything in this house he needed but what was standing in front of him. If he couldn't have that, he could be good and gone before Jay could even lower his supercilious eyebrows.

He turned his back on the door. Call it public service. He'd make an effort on behalf of the next guy who fell for the kind of intensity Jay could dish out before learning that he wasn't ever going to be more than a little challenge Jay set for himself. "You know when I got the offer for this job, you were the first person I wanted to tell. Not because I need outside approval, or because I was trying to prove something. But because God knows why, I fell for you and I wanted you to be excited for me."

"Shane."

He wished Jay wouldn't say his name like that. It was easier doing this if he could tell himself that Jay barely even noticed he was here.

He wasn't sure he'd ever heard such a gentle tone in Jay's voice before. Not even in bed. "I know what you want me to say, but I can't tell you something I don't believe in."

"Right. I remember. 'I Don't Believe In Love'. You and

213

Queensrÿche. Nice ink." Shane ripped his shirt over his head. "Man, of all the stupid things I've done—and I've done a lot, I've never done anything like this." He turned around to show Jay his back.

Silence. Had Shane really thought it would matter? "Can you read it?"

"Yes."

More silence.

Shane shifted his shoulder. "I see what you mean about stupid impulses now."

"No you don't." Jay yanked him around, spun him until they were face to face. His skin was that dead coral grey it had been the day they'd met. His eyes were flat and empty.

Shane's skin prickled like it had when they'd come up and the boat had been missing. Because as bad a mistake as he'd thought getting that tattoo was, he knew he was about to find out it was a much bigger one.

"This." Jay shoved his inked arm under Shane's nose. "This wasn't some stupid teenage rebellion. It wasn't because I listened to *Operation: Mindcrime* so many times I can still hear every beat of every track in my head." He grabbed Shane's hand and put his fingers over the long black point that ran from Jay's wrist to the middle of his forearm. "Feel that. That's why I have this fucking tattoo."

Shane ran his fingers over the ridge, still trying to understand. Tattoos were raised sometimes, especially when they were brand new, as he had good reason to know, but this one was old. The needles didn't go that deep. There something under there. A scar. A long slash between the bones, thick with bumps from multiple stitches.

Jesus.

Shane swallowed hard. "Why?"

Jay tried to pull his arm back, but Shane kept it, fingers gliding over that old deep wound, wishing like hell he could take back a lot of shit he'd said, wishing even more he could go back and fix whatever had made Jay tear a hole in himself like that.

Jay let him keep the arm, but he looked away. "I told you you couldn't understand Korean culture. When I was sixteen, some other kid and I, we sucked each other off. And then he freaked out and told his parents and his parents called my parents."

As much as Shane didn't want to hear it, he was afraid to do anything that would stop Jay's story, but Shane's thumb couldn't stop rubbing across that thick line of pain under the ink. How could he have not noticed it before?

"I thought there'd be a lot of screaming and crying. Maybe even an exorcism. They're Catholic," Jay went on, a little bit of his usual self in that wry explanation. "But they sat me down in the kitchen. I remember every fleck and mark and groove in the table because it's all I could look at.

"They said, well, my mother was the one to talk. My father couldn't even face me. She said quite calmly that she knew this other boy was lying. That their son could never be anything disgusting like that. That she would rather her son be dead than do anything like that."

Shane pressed his lips together tight before what he was thinking came rushing out. Christ. People should have to have some kind of test before they were allowed to breed. How the hell could someone say that to her kid?

He thought about how his own family had reacted. His mom had claimed she'd known all along and had just been waiting for him to say something. Josh had offered to beat up whoever had "turned" him, Megan tried to fix him up with

215

dates. And they all loved him.

Jay looked up now. Shane held on to his arm and waited.

"So Sunday when they went to church, I stayed home sick. And I was."

Shane didn't know how anybody could stand there all clear-eyed and tell this story. The blank look on Jay's face was enough to put tears in Shane's eyes.

"I knew there wasn't any way not to be what my parents considered a disgusting failure. So I figured I could still give them what they wanted. I did such a good job on the first wrist, I never needed to start the second one. Couldn't even hold the knife.

"My sister had a headache and she came home early. Actually, she told me later she wanted to check on me. But she got me to the hospital."

Thank God someone in Jay's family had loved him.

"I honestly don't know if my parents would have bothered. They never talked about it, and when they did, it was my 'accident'. I didn't want to talk about it either so when it had healed enough, I got this to cover it." He pulled his arm free.

Shane let it go and took the whole Jay package instead, pulling him into a tight hug. "God, Jay. I'm so sorry. So fucking sorry. I never would have gotten—"

"It's all right." Jay pushed free. "But, Shane—"

And the sound of his name in that calm voice, the one that had just explained how his parents had tried to fucking kill him when he was a kid made Shane want to sob like a baby. And it was a damned good thing there were probably ten thousand Kim families in Orlando, because Shane could see himself going down there and leveling the kind of justice neither Christ nor Buddha would approve of.

Jay wasn't finished. "It's why I know."

"Know what?"

"You know it too. You've been there. You die and that's it. I'm not talking about religion, just biology. I've been there, I've seen that moment so many times and there's nothing. Just something alive and then something dead. All that stuff about love and souls and bonds and connections, it's just how people get themselves through it. It's all in your head."

"What a pile of crap. Of course it's all in your head, what the hell kind of doctor are you? Everything's in your head. But that doesn't make it less real. It's not my heart that's in love with you, it's my head."

Jay stepped back, face closed. Shane might as well have told him they were out of eggs.

He leaned down because closed off or not, Jay was going to hear this. "And you can't believe that because if your big fucking brain can't prove it in some lab experiment, then what I feel—hell what I've been feeling since I watched you try to make friends with a moray eel—doesn't exist. Doesn't mean anything. Well, it does. And I am sorry. Sorrier than I have ever been because I need it."

"No you don't need it. You tell yourself you need it. All you need is food, air, water and shelter."

"Christ, even my truck needs more than that. And you know what? If that's the case, I got no reason to be here. Got all that covered on my own. Got enough in the bank to buy anything I need. Hell, I can even manage to get laid on my own. Or did you really think I flew two thousand miles for your dick?"

Jay stepped back again. Was that the face people saw when he came in to tell them, "Sorry, we did everything we could but the patient didn't make it?" That mask that didn't let a hint of the funny, sweet guy Shane loved come through at all. That guy

217

would never put an afghan over his drunk boyfriend who was passed out on the porch.

"So what happens now?" Jay asked.

"I don't know. But I know I can't go through what I went through last night again. I'm not a fighter, Jay. I don't have the patience for it."

"But I'm not going to San Diego."

"That's not what this is about. I never would have thought you'd leave if you'd just tell me what you're feeling. And you can't. So I can't."

"I thought we worked this out. Why are you changing the rules?"

If Jay's voice had anything to it, anything like what Shane had heard on that reef in Belize, the rough desperate urgency that had kept him alive, Shane would have never thought about walking through that door for good again. But there was still nothing.

"We never set any rules, remember?"

"And you've made up your mind."

"You're the one with the made-up mind. Let me ask you something, Dr. Kim. If we're all nothing but slaves to our cells, why would you have risked your continued existence to save my life out there? You could have been stung too, and we'd both have died. You could have drowned trying to drag me to the reef. You want to tell me that was just your job?"

"You're going to hold my saving your life against me?"

Shane shook his head. "I'll go you one better. If it's all biology, why the hell are we gay? How does that make sense? Biology would make you want pussy over cock, and then you could make your parents happy."

Shane wished the words back as soon as he said them. He

218

always did go too far. And he got his reaction all right, just not any kind that made him think he was going to be spending another night in this house, in that bed with Jay.

Kim walked over to the door and unhooked Shane's keys.

"If I'm really making you that miserable, why the hell are you still standing here?" Jay tossed the keys and Shane caught them. Jay hadn't thrown them hard, but somehow Shane's palm still stung.

"The door's not locked. Why don't you go through it before you start blaming me for liver damage because you can't wait a few hours to ask me a simple question? Because *that* is what this is all about."

And Jay walked the fuck away. Shane squeezed the keys tight enough to dig into his skin, and went out the front door.

Chapter Eighteen

After the door shut behind Shane—with a click not a slam, which somehow sounded a lot more final than if he'd left in a rage—Kim picked up the ticket from the kitchen counter and took it back to his desk. There was a check there from Shane, made out for three thousand dollars. A neon pink sticky note had neat block printing on it.

"Guess it didn't work out. This should cover anything I owe you."

He looked at the date on the check. Yesterday.

Nice to know Shane had already given up. He could have said something and spared Kim having to spit out that painful confession. Could have just left the check and the note and the plane ticket in a stack on the desk and vanished.

Kim's fingers twitched, as if he could feel the paper tearing in his hands as he tore it into bits, but he wasn't sure which he wanted to tear into more: the check or the ticket. He put them both together and remembered that impulsive physical actions in the wake of emotional stress were rarely as satisfying as their conception. He rubbed his wrist. He thought after all this time he wouldn't need such a visceral reminder. The check and the ticket went back into his bill file.

He looked in the dresser they shared, in the hall closet. Shane's clothes were still there. Razor. Toothbrush. Fruit-scented conditioner. He hadn't bothered to pack but he'd stopped to write out a three thousand dollar check.

Kim was putting the bottle of acetaminophen away when he saw the rubber tree plant his mother had given him when he moved to Jacksonville. Shane liked it and had moved it out onto the lanai, next to the glider.

Kim reached down and picked it up, not really conscious of the weight of plant and soil and earthenware. In fact, he'd never felt less connected to his body. Not even when everything was draining out of him on the bathroom floor of his parents' house, when everything got black and cold and empty. He watched himself lift the plant and hurl it through the screen window. It went pretty far, bouncing and rolling halfway across the yard before plant and pot parted ways.

Now that he had a nice big hole, the uncomfortable plastic chairs followed, one at a time. They bounced, too, but one leg snapped off with a loud crack. A physical expression of anger was actually kind of satisfying, provided it was directed at furniture and not himself. A gecko crawled out from the space where the plant had been, blinked and oiled its way up the stucco wall.

Kim felt the irrational wish to apologize to it. He didn't even try for the glider. Just sank down on the floor next to it and caught his breath. With the link between body and brain reinstated, his hands hurt. The knuckles were scraped, though he couldn't remember hitting anything.

His phone sounded with the ring tone from the hospital, so he climbed to his feet and answered it. "Kim."

"Hey. Listen. You got me in serious shit, you know."

"Aaron. What are you doing calling from the hospital phone?"

"I got patched through. I knew that way you'd pick it up."

"And now I'm hanging up."

Kim heard Joey in the background saying, "Give me the goddamned phone, Aaron." The mental image of Aaron holding it well out of Joey's reach and him jumping for it like their puppy after a treat would have made Kim laugh, if he didn't feel like he was stuck on one of those night dives with no flashlight. And no Shane.

As much as misery might love company, Kim could use the distraction. "What did I do?"

"You told me you and your cowboy were free to fuck around. So when he called and asked where he could get laid, I told him. And now I've got an armful of pissed-off blond." Aaron's voice dropped to a whisper. "You know it's true, Kim. If Joey ain't happy, ain't nobody happy. So tell him that everything's fine, okay?"

As a distraction, this sucked. Everything wasn't fine. Because that inky cold sank all the way into his bones, froze all the fluid in his cells, and as much as he tried to retreat into his head, remind himself that such sensations were nothing more than a visceral response to stress, he couldn't bury the feeling that this was what it was going to be like for the rest of his life. Unless he did something to fix it.

"I'm afraid you and your blond are going to have to work this out on your own, Aaron. Goodbye." He slammed the phone shut.

Kim parked the Jetta as close as he could get to the marshy shore and still be on firm ground, locked it and walked toward the cluster of people at the shoreline just past the new Marine Research Institute of Jacksonville University. His Scuba Cowboy/Indiana Jones was easy to pick out, and not just because of his hair. He was the only one in a wide-brimmed hat and a wet suit.

Since most of the students had mesh bags slung over their shoulders and were edging off, Kim concluded the field class was almost over. Instead of the river offering a few degrees of respite, it was hotter down here, the ground steaming, a smell far too close to perforated bowels coming out of the mud.

Shane wrapped things up. "So if you have any questions, email or stop by Thursday, two to four."

The teenagers slogged off through the swampy grass. Shane turned to pack away his own gear and Kim came up behind him.

"I have a question."

Shane spun around. In that outfit, he should have looked ridiculous, but Kim was just glad to see those blue eyes widen in surprise.

The lids came down, halfway, sexy and lazy all at once. Kim's vomeronasal organ was doing battle with his olfactory bulb, trying to push pheromones over stench.

"What?" Shane stretched the word out, head tilted. If he tucked his hair behind his ears, Kim was going to be on his knees begging.

"You said you couldn't go through what you went through last night again."

"Yeah."

"Did it involve feeling like you were so empty inside it hurt? Like you were watching your blood swirl down a drain, only worse this time because you couldn't blame the biggest mistake of your life on being a stupid teenager?"

"Jay..." Shane stepped toward him, mesh bag falling to his feet with a clunk.

"I feel things. I do. And when they're up here..." he tapped his temple, "...they make sense. But when I try to put them in words, it comes out wrong. So it's easier not to say anything."

"Try."

Kim swallowed and tried to free up his throat. He remembered sitting on the floor of his hall in shock. Holding that letter and picturing Shane and knowing he couldn't have both. As soon as he understood the choice, it had been easy. "About San Diego. It took me exactly three minutes to pick up the phone and tell them thanks but no thanks."

"I know how much you wanted it."

"You have no idea."

"I would if you'd tell me."

"I'm trying." Kim ground his teeth together and gave it another shot. Because just like then, he knew there was only once choice. Picking the right one had never been a problem. Explaining it was a different matter. Give him a multiple choice test any day. "I don't like not knowing the answer. And I don't like having to get answers from other people. But if you say that this is what love feels like, I'll take your word for it."

"That's a start."

"So love mostly feels like being seasick?"

"No." Shane cupped Kim's jaw with his hand. "Mostly it feels like this."

The kiss was tentative, like they'd never done it before, like they weren't sure it was what both of them wanted. But the first slow lick of Shane's tongue against Kim's started a thaw. Shane seemed to move through him, like warm clear water from the Gulf. Kim stopped swimming and just floated.

Shane lifted his head. He was watching Kim's face closely, eyes wary. "I need some rules this time."

"Okay." But Shane didn't say anything. Didn't make a

single request. Kim took a breath. "I promise I will try to tell you what I'm thinking. Right now I'm thinking that it stinks here. How can you possibly stand it?"

"Welcome to the glamorous world of archaeology. Golden idols, magic gems and hidden tombs, all the time. But I don't need a play by play, all right? Just keep me in the loop."

"All right. But I need a promise from you too. I'm always going to need time to figure things out. And I don't want one of those things I'm thinking to be that you're always already halfway out the door."

"I'm not."

"Shane, I got the check. Hell of a goodbye, but maybe you should have left the date off."

"Yeah. I was pretty pissed last night." Shane smeared a little mud on his cheek as he pushed his hat back. He nodded. "I promise. You've got all the time you need. I'm not going anywhere."

Since he was trying something new, Kim put into words something that had been bugging him for months. "I know that stuff about cattle barons was bullshit, but where did you get all this money?"

"Settlement from Sea Magic's insurance. Didn't they make you an offer?"

"The lawyers are still talking."

"So now what?" Shane asked.

"Now we go where you can get out of that wet suit, Scuba Cowboy turned Indiana Jones."

Shane laughed. "I think I like *baby* better."

"I'll try to remember."

Shane pointed at the building behind them. "My office is— well you can't exactly see it because it doesn't have windows on the river, but—"

"I was thinking like your truck. It's closer."

"And a hundred and forty degrees inside it. C'mon, I'll give you a tour."

Kim picked up one of the bags and followed Shane through the grass. There was something of a path. "Hey. Were you very attached to that rubber tree plant?"

"It's a plant, Jay."

"Okay. Well, I threw it through the screen."

"How very irrational and emotional of you, Mr. Spock."

"God, not *Star Trek* again. Talk about moralizing."

Shane rinsed off his gear and stowed it in a locked storage room that was already starting to reek of mold. He brushed off the dried mud on his legs and scraped it off a pair of sneakers that looked like he'd found them in a landfill.

The rest of the building smelled fresh and new. Unfinished even. As they took the elevator up and walked down the hall, Kim saw panels still missing from the ceiling, a rolled carpet and a doorway made out of sheet plastic.

Shane's office didn't have a nice plaque like some, just his name and office hours on a plain white printout. Kim was going to buy him one. Etched on brass. Permanent.

Shane unlocked the door and held it open for Kim.

He pointed back at the sign. "Shouldn't it say Dr. Dr. McCormack?"

"Shut up."

The office was neat, but half finished like the rest of the building. Kim inspected the framed diplomas on the walls.

"They're real. My mom sent them. We're supposed to display them."

"Two doctorates. My mother would be so happy. If you didn't have a dick."

"I'm not giving that up. Not even for my mother." Shane unzipped the neoprene and pushed it off his shoulders. "Are you ever going to tell them?"

"Don't ask don't tell has been working better for me than the military for sixteen years. They can wait until they get a copy of our marriage license in the mail. Which given the political situation in Florida will probably be another sixteen years."

"Man. When you uncork, you uncork."

"I said I'd try."

The expression on Shane's face shifted to one of shock. And then happiness, blue eyes clear and warm. "Wait. Back up. Did you just propose to me?"

Kim walked over and pulled the wet suit down to Shane's hips. Reaching up, he slid a finger gently across the letters on Shane's back. "You are carrying my name on your skin. I probably should make an honest man out of you."

Shane laughed, the sound chasing away the last of that hollow feeling.

He backed Shane into his desk. "Did you lock the door?"

"Yeah."

Kim yanked the neoprene down over Shane's hips, taking the swim trunks with it. "Baby." The word still felt funny on Kim's lips, but like having a boyfriend, and eating lasagna out of a measuring cup, he'd get used to it.

Shane grinned. "Yeah?"

"Leave the hat on."

About the Author

K.A. Mitchell discovered the magic of writing at an early age when she learned that a carefully crayoned note of apology sent to the kitchen in a toy truck would earn her a reprieve from banishment to her room. Her career as a spin control artist was cut short when her family moved to a two-story house, and her trucks would not roll safely down the stairs. Around the same time, she decided that Chip and Ken made a much cuter couple than Ken and Barbie and was perplexed when invitations to play Barbie dropped off. An unnamed number of years later, she's happy to find other readers and writers who like to play in her world.

To learn more about K.A. Mitchell, please visit www.kamitchell.com. Send an email to K.A. Mitchell at authorKAMitchell@gmail.com.

Truth. Lies. A century-old mystery. What a tangled web...

Love Like Ghosts
© *2009 Ally Blue*
A *Bay City Paranormal Investigations* story.

At age eleven, Adrian Broussard accidentally used his mind to open a portal to another dimension. Now, ten years later, he's successfully harnessed his strong psychokinetic abilities. In the process, he's learned the lessons which have become the guiding principles of his life. Absolute truth. Absolute control. Always.

Sticking to his personal code of ethics has never been a problem, until two chance meetings—one with a hundred-year-old ghost, one with a handsome, very-much-alive man—turn his orderly existence upside down.

Having grown up in a family of paranormal investigators, Adrian is intrigued by the spirit of Lyndon Groome and determined to solve the mystery of his death. Greg Woodhall, however, affects Adrian in unpredictable ways. Not only does his every touch challenge Adrian's hard-won control over his abilities, his company quickly becomes a light in Adrian's lonely life.

As the mystery surrounding Lyndon's death turns sinister, Adrian's relationship with Greg deepens into something serious. Something Adrian wants to keep. But intimacy isn't as easy as honesty, and when the heart's involved, the line between right and wrong can blur.

Warning: This book contains a gory ghost, a haunted castle, nerdy college parties and gay sex enhanced by psychic powers.

Available now in ebook and print from Samhain Publishing.

*He followed all the rules...until one man showed him
a dozen ways to break them.*

An Improper Holiday
© 2009 K.A. Mitchell

As second son to an earl, Ian Stanton has always done the proper thing. Obeyed his elders, studied diligently, and dutifully accepted the commission his father purchased for him in the Fifty-Second Infantry Division. The one glaring, shameful, marvelous exception: Nicholas Chatham, heir to the Marquess of Carleigh.

Before Ian took his position in His Majesty's army, he and Nicky consummated two years of physical and emotional discovery. Their inexperience created painful consequences that led Ian to the conviction that their unnatural desires were never meant to be indulged.

Five years later, wounded in body and plagued by memories of what happened between them, Ian is sent to carry out his older brother's plans for a political alliance with Nicky's father. Their sister Charlotte is the bargaining piece.

Nicky never believed that what he and Ian felt for each other was wrong and he has a plan to make things right. Getting Ian to Carleigh is but the first step. Now Nicky has only twelve nights to convince Ian that happiness is not the price of honor and duty, but its reward.

Warning: Just thinking about reading this book in 1814 could get you hanged, so the men in this book who enjoy m/m interaction of an intimately penetrative nature are in a hell of a lot of trouble.

Available now in ebook from Samhain Publishing.
Available in the print anthology To All a (Very Sexy) Good Night..

HOT STUFF

Discover Samhain!
THE HOTTEST NEW PUBLISHER ON THE PLANET

Romance, fantasy, mystery, thriller, mainstream and more—Samhain has more selection, hotter authors, and everything's available in ebook.

Pick your favorite, sit back, and enjoy the ride! Hot stuff indeed.

LaVergne, TN USA
14 January 2011
212444LV00008B/3/P